In the Shadow of the Strip

WESTERN LITERATURE SERIES

T0163503

In the Shadow of the Strip
Las Vegas Stories

EDITED BY

Richard Logsdon

Todd Scott Moffett

Tina D. Eliopulos

University of Nevada Press ▲▲ Reno & Las Vegas

Western Literature Series
University of Nevada Press, Reno, Nevada 89557 USA
Copyright © 2003 by University of Nevada Press
All rights reserved
Manufactured in the United States of America

Library of Congress Cataloging-in-Publication Data
In the shadow of the strip : Las Vegas stories / [compiled by] Richard
Logsdon, Todd Scott Moffett, and Tina D. Eliopulos.
p. cm. — (Western literature series)
ISBN 0-87417-549-6 (pbk. : alk. paper)
1. Las Vegas (Nev.)—Fiction. 2. Short stories, American—Nevada—Las Vegas.
I. Logsdon, Richard, 1948–   II. Moffett, Todd Scott, 1963–
III. Eliopulos, Tina D. (Tina Dawn), 1963–   IV. Series.
PS574.L37 I5 2003
813'.010832793135—dc21   2002156542

The paper used in this book meets the requirements of American
National Standard for Information Sciences—Permanence of Paper
for Printed Library Materials, ANSI Z.48-1984. Binding
materials were selected for strength and durability.

First Printing
12 11 10 09 08 07 06 05 04 03
5 4 3 2 1

*To Louis John Eliopulos, who loved Las Vegas and all its stories.
His love and life will be a part of the city lights always.*

—T.D.E.

Contents

Preface

The Making of *In the Shadow of the Strip*

A transplanted Idahoan, I've lived in Las Vegas with my wife for more than twenty-five years, and I'm still not sure that I know the place. I do remember waking up to news that Lefty Rosenthal's car had been firebombed the night before. I remember the MGM fire. When my mother was still alive and coming down to Las Vegas four times a year, I had the opportunity to see just about every major performer and every major show on the Strip. I have read *Literary Las Vegas* and recognized in its narratives the city I came to years ago. Yet, Las Vegas's growth has now pushed it beyond easy definition. The city's recent phenomenal development may have given it a new identity that takes it way beyond such labels as "adult Disneyland," "Sin City," "Lost Wages," or "the gambling capital of the world."

Certainly within the past ten or fifteen years, Las Vegas has struggled to move beyond Bugsy Siegel's vision of the city as a paradise for gangsters, and at times it has become what *Time* magazine described several years back as the all-American family city of the future. But credit must be given where credit is due, and Mr. Siegel did succeed in providing a dark yet dazzling cultural framework whose presence cannot be denied, regardless of how many landmarks the city destroys.

So where, I wonder, does this leave us? Admittedly, the presence of the relatively new suburbs of Summerlin and Green Valley and the strategic placement of malls in southern Nevada might signal to the rest of the country that Las Vegas is becoming just like any other American city. As the city expands toward two million people, it seems to do so in an attempt to pull away from its somewhat legendary past, popularized in such films as *Casino* and *Showgirls*. Yet, if literature is at all about truth, then the stories contained in this anthology suggest that, in spite of its growth, Las Vegas may not have moved very far from its core. Accordingly, Las Vegas remains a desert oasis that sustains itself in large part by wrapping visitors and residents in a tangle of dreams and illusions that make this anything but a typical American city.

Somewhat in line with traditional views of the city, several of the stories suggest that illusion is almost interchangeable with reality in this environment. In David Kranes's "The Fish Magician," for instance, illusion blurs with reality as a struggling Strip magician accidentally loses one of his participants in a disappearing act. In Andrew Kiraly's "The Funniest Thing You Said All Night," Las Vegas becomes a symbol for Jason's dreams and failures. In perhaps the most subtle piece in the collection, David Scott's "Golfers," Earnie and Sandov find a dream world within the dream world of Las Vegas. Their preoccupation with golf blinds them to the beauty of the natural landscape, which becomes one more fanciful backdrop for adults living out their fantasies.

In many of the stories, Las Vegas is treated so ironically that one wonders what constitutes the real city. Satire permeates John L. Smith's "Big-City Detective," which is told from the point of view of Lucky Jack Brown from Baker, California, an outcast who finds in Las Vegas, a city of "freaks," the home he's always looked for. The marginally psychotic Roy Stuart in Felicia Campbell's "The God Gambler" uses his newfound faith to justify and fuel his gambling addiction in a city in which sincere religious conviction and the vices associated with gambling are incompatible. In Thomas A. Porter's "Easy Driving," the narrator's lifelong goal of traveling 100,000 miles will be fulfilled somewhere between San Francisco and Las Vegas, a city built on winning by getting the right numbers. Mr. Biondi's nihilism in German Santanilla's "Mr. Biondi and the New Dispensation" easily blends with an environment in which nothing seems substantial, in which everything is an extension of the delusional world of Las Vegas. And in Dayvid Figler's "Bowling with the Christ Child," Las Vegas is less a city than it is a realm of existence whose absence of boundaries makes plausible, within a fictional context, an evening of bowling with the Savior of humanity, who (incidentally) is not very good at this pastime. At their core, these stories suggest that Las Vegas is more an illusion, more a state of mind, than anything else.

Several stories do move beyond the illusory side of Las Vegas to touch upon a darkness contained in, yet lying beneath, the city's dreams. In Matthew O'Brien's "Insufficient Funds," Nick Costello's obsession with betting on college sports is an addictive, irrevocable fact of his life: he can no more make himself stop thinking about numbers, statistics, and betting than he can command himself to stop breathing. In H. Lee Barnes's "The Run," addiction merges with mild psychosis as Luther seeks signs assuring him that he is indeed always on the verge of making his fortune in Las Vegas. A more comical, even satirical story, José Skinner's "Naked City" reveals a character whose vision is blurred by fascination bordering on an obsession induced by the artificial environment. Skinner's character Ernie has been retired from the Signal Communications and Aerospace Technology plant in Henderson; his fascination with sexual fantasy, an effect of living in a city that caters to adult entertainment, has finally distorted his ability to view people around him accurately. Robert Dodge's "Las Vegas Courtship" is a finely crafted piece about two losers—a compulsive gambler and a wannabe showgirl—who are devastated by the failure of their dreams in Las Vegas but who redeem each other by falling in love and deciding to spend their lives together. Willy Parker of Richard Logsdon's "The Night Uncle Willy's Car Caught on Fire on the I-95" finds no escape from the city's numbing darkness that claims his life and soul. And, in Michael Ventura's "You Saw Me Crying in the Chapel," Virginia's identity crisis, her sense of the disappearance of her own true identity, reflects Las Vegas's own muddied attempts to redefine what it is.

What we have in *In the Shadow of the Strip* is a collage of well-crafted, fictional impressions of a city that seems to be moving in several different directions simultaneously. Certainly, the Las Vegas depicted in Felicia Campbell's story is as much a presence now as it was fifteen years ago. The main characters in the stories by Barnes, O'Brien, and Skinner are representative of people who are and have been fixtures in a community that, in an effort to separate people from their money in any way possible, has catered to the vices soundly condemned by this country's Puritan founders. But the stories here also suggest that in Las Vegas a new, perhaps more complex identity is emerging. This anthology is offered as an attempt to make sense of this continually changing city and illuminate its always enigmatic soul.

RICHARD LOGSDON

Acknowledgments

"The Run," by H. Lee Barnes, originally appeared in *Connecticut Review* (Fall 2000).

"Las Vegas Courtship," by Robert Dodge, originally appeared in *Las Vegan City Magazine* (April 1978).

"Bowling with the Christ Child," by Dayvid Figler, originally appeared in *Red Rock Review* (Winter 1999).

"The Funniest Thing You Said All Night," by Andrew Kiraly, originally appeared in *Red Rock Review* (Summer 2001).

"The Fish Magician," by David Kranes, originally appeared in *Great Basin* (Summer 1997).

"The Night Uncle Willy's Car Caught on Fire on the I-95," by Richard Logsdon, originally appeared in *San Francisco Salvo* (Spring 1999).

"Mr. Biondi and the New Dispensation," by German Santanilla, originally appeared in *Chance* (Spring 1999).

"You Saw Me Crying in the Chapel," by Michael Ventura, originally appeared in *Red Rock Review* (Summer 1998).

The Run

H. LEE BARNES

Luther drove I-15 south. Behind, against the backdrop of a purple sky, the city lights blazed. He laid his foot to the accelerator and didn't look back at the all-too-familiar skyline—Sin City, Counterfeit Eden, Postmodern Gomorrah—all the clichés and more he couldn't think of at the moment. He could almost hear the chatter at a craps table and the compelling bark of a stickman calling dice. He could almost smell the cigarette smoke and feel cards in his hands, taste saliva form as he placed a bet. There was something about holding cards and hoping. Put it out of your mind. If only, he thought. He murmured and slipped an Eagles CD in the player.

He held the steering wheel steady until he reached the Blue Diamond cutoff. There he pulled off the interstate and into the potholed parking lot of a 76 truck stop, where he parked in a spot near an outside pay phone. His fingers trembled as he dropped thirty-five cents in the slot. He took a deep breath and dialed. He was scared, had every reason to be. The line buzzed three times before the receiver clicked and a man's nasal voice said hello.

"Hy, this is Luther."

"Luther. Yeah, Luther. You got my money?"

Lie to your mother, but never to a shylock. Luther knew the rules. He had something less than a hundred dollars in bills and a jar of loose change, mostly quarters, in the glove box. Hy's money? He remembered the last time he'd called. His debt was already seven thousand and he was paying a hundred and twenty a week just to keep the shylock off his back. He'd fallen behind. His situation seemed like some cliché out of a bad movie, but doesn't everyone's?

"Not yet," he said. "I was wondering . . . could you give me more time? I mean, it's not like we haven't done business before, years now, and haven't I always been good?"

"Eleven thousand, Luther. You stopped paying the vig. You've cost me time."

"Ten thousand," Luther said.

"I had to hire help," Hy said. "That kind of help is expensive."

A semi rattled up to the fuel pumps and drowned out the sound of Hy's voice. Luther looked in the direction of the sixteen-wheeler and sighed. Men had been to his apartment. He'd seen them from the parking lot knocking on his door—large men, one black, one not, but they were the same in every other way. He knew the type, and he knew what they were after and who'd sent them. They liked their work.

"Where are you, Luther?"

Luther cupped the phone, trying to think of a good lie. He couldn't come up with one. He swallowed and said, "In twelve years I've paid over a hundred thousand in vig."

"This is now. Where are you?"

Luther nodded as if Hy were in front of him. "I'll have it in two days," he said.

There was a silent moment, then Hy coughed into the mouthpiece. After clearing his throat, he said, "Guys like you play to lose. Tomorrow before noon."

This time Luther was playing to win. "Hy, I'm not stiffing you. I can come up with it," he said, though it was a bald lie.

"Uh-huh, and I suppose you'll make a score. Easier to get money back from a junkie. At least they steal. Why don't you steal? Man behind a blackjack game has prospects."

Prospects? Luther thought. Less than a hundred dollars, pocket change, clothes, and a vague destination. But the money would do him better in California than eleven thousand would a shylock in Vegas. "Two days, Hy. Give me two days."

"It's nine thirty. You got till noon."

The line went dead.

Luther clasped the receiver for a moment as if clutching a bar of hope. In a single call he'd severed himself from his shylock . . . and from casinos as well. At least that was his intention. Well, what's done is . . . but he didn't feel confident as he lowered the receiver into its cradle. Now, he thought with resignation, California was where he'd get it together. There were places to hide and to find work, real work. Maybe in time, when he was established, he'd see if

Celeste wanted to give it a try again. Aside from his gambling, things had been fine. He was feeling better as he gassed the car.

Heading west, traffic was light, but the opposing lane was a ceaseless string of headlights flowing east, mile upon mile of California pilgrims making the Friday night trek to Vegas. Luther looked in the rearview mirror to watch the neon glow shrink and noticed the dim outline of clothes piled in the backseat. Those along with a few sheets and towels in the trunk and a valise with photos and a never fired .32 Star automatic comprised the sum of his worldly possessions. Everything else—stereo, TV, microwave, watches, jewelry— had long been sacrificed to pawnshops after Celeste had walked out the door. How many times had he told her he'd make a score and they could leave? But Vegas didn't affect her the way it did him. Why leave? That was her.

Luther popped a Moody Blues album in the CD player. He'd not shown at work at seven as scheduled. Nor had he called in. A termination slip with his name on it awaited him and he would never see it. He'd be the talk of the dealers' room for a couple of days—until someone asked, "Did you hear about Luther?" and the answer was "Luther who?" Dead to the memory in a week.

As he neared the Baker grade, he passed a Toyota sedan with Nevada plates. He didn't catch the letters, but the numbers read 777. He wondered if the plate had brought the driver luck. "What difference?" he muttered, and reached to change the CD. The clock read 11:11, P.M. He swallowed as he loaded Bob Seger's *Night Moves*. Taking a deep breath, he leaned back, gripped the wheel with both hands and stared ahead. That was when the Toyota overtook him and passed again. As the rear bumper came into Luther's headlights, he noted the plate was 777 WIN. Jesus! He floored the accelerator and passed the car. He had to put it behind him.

A few minutes later he reached the Baker turnoff. He didn't need gas, but decided coffee and a short rest would do him good. He pulled into the parking lot of Kay's, an unremarkable calorie café like so many on the roadside from L.A. to Vegas. He grabbed a handful of quarters from the glove box. The café was lit like an operating room. He followed the directions of a sign and found the toilets down a back hallway. As he stood before the urinal, he noticed on the wall a few inches from his nose a note scratched with a fingernail file or penknife. It read, "Play with Don at the Sands. Can't win a hand." Luther closed his eyes and urinated.

He sat at the counter. The waitress asked if he was heading to Vegas. He said he wasn't. She told him that was too bad, that he could make a bet for her if he was.

"You'd trust me to make the bet," he asked, "and pay you if you won?"

"What difference does it make, darlin'? It's the idea I could win, isn't it?"

He pushed his cup toward her for a refill. "San Diego's my destination," he said as if it had been a lifelong plan.

After downing two cups of bitter but strong coffee, he left, ready to take on the interstate again. As he turned onto the roadway, he wasn't feeling quite as sure about matters as he had just two hours before, but he was determined. Barstow, Victorville, then south to San Diego. Surely he'd find work, some small thing, waiting tables or the like. At least he'd decided on his destination. He would make it. He punched the gas pedal and got up to cruising speed. The white lines and shoulder of the road blurred. He tried not to think of Celeste, but found himself remembering her as she was the night she'd first walked into the pit at the Maxim. He'd looked up from his 21 game to see her brush her hair back with her fingers and knew he had to have her. Two weeks later they'd met after work and gambled at the Hilton. She'd dropped thirty dollars and stopped. He'd gone on a tear, piling up stacks of chips as she watched. Before he knew it, he'd gotten seven thousand ahead. But the run had stopped as unpredictably as it had started. Celeste had urged him to quit, but he didn't until his piles had shrunk to twenty-two hundred dollars and she'd warned him she would leave without him. He'd taken her arm and walked her to the jewelry store, where he'd bought her a ring with a fire opal the size of her thumbnail. She'd said he was crazy, then had driven him to her apartment, where she bathed him with a sponge to get the smell of the casino off before they made love.

A terrible hunch was coming on. Signs flashed everywhere—roadside markers, license plates, numbers on the sides of semis that rolled by. His heart thudded. His hands felt clammy. He brushed his fingers through his hair, tried not to think about the feeling. Pictured himself on the beach in San Diego. Yes, San Diego!

He recalled a player stepping up to his game one night six years before. The man, in his late forties, had seemed nervous. Luther had asked if it was his first time out. "No," the man said, "I've been coming for years. Why?" Luther explained that he appeared nervous. "Oh. That's not it. A hunch told me you're the one." He sat down and turned a hundred-dollar bill into sixty thousand. Hunches? Luther shook his head.

His mouth was dry. He couldn't swallow. As he passed Barstow, he saw a sign advertising a Motel 21. No, a Motel 6, he thought. But it was Motel 21, for there was a second sign that said it was back one exit. His hands and feet went cold. Although it was September and seventy-five degrees, he turned on the heater. How long had he been listening to Bob Seger? He opened his CD case and took out another. As he rose up from switching the discs, the odometer turned over 77,077. He slammed his hands on the steering wheel.

After that he seemed to float inside the car. Nothing seemed clear, and everywhere he looked, numbers screamed at him. He was in the middle of nowhere going in the opposite direction from where all that spoke to him told him to go. He forced himself to think of a better time, of Celeste and him in a hotel in La Jolla, where a bottle of wine sat on a table and the drapes were drawn open as they ate in the dark, sitting across from one another naked. They talked of marriage. He intended to propose, but didn't. The next day they went to Tijuana, where he lost eight hundred betting on jai alai. They paid for the room with her credit card and drove to Vegas in silence. Had that been a better time? Had there been a *better* time?

Now his hands were shaking and his stomach churned. The sensation was all too familiar. The risk rush, he'd named it. He had first experienced the feeling when he was ten and living outside Paso Robles near some vineyards, which were surrounded by an electric fence to discourage livestock. He used to place his palms on either side of the wire and gradually bring them toward one another until he could feel the twelve-volt force field. Each time he would give in to the temptation to see how close he could come without touching the wire or getting shocked. In time he was shocked, but that didn't stop him from doing it again. Then, as now, the rush came on like a physical illness—chills, fever. He thought about a guy named Don. What did he look like?

Maybe it would help to see how far San Diego was. He pulled over to look at the map. His fingers trembled as he turned on the overhead light and unfolded the map. He started to calculate distance. Twenty-eight miles east of Victorville. San Diego is . . . He saw a passing truck, its side painted with dice—two sixes, boxcars— and tossed the map aside without folding it, then jammed the accelerator to the floorboard, leaving a strip of rubber on the paved shoulder.

He couldn't ignore the hunch.

At a crossover he turned the car around and looked for a seam in the oncoming traffic. He fell in behind a procession of taillights that seemed to lead nonstop to the Atlantic. What if the sensation passed before he got back to Vegas? What if he was misreading it? He felt a terrible sense of dread and a desire to do something wild to overcome it—honk his horn, steer onto the shoulder and start passing cars. What was going on? There was no good answer.

As if of its own will, the car drifted to the right and slowed. When he came to a dirt road, the car seemed to pull itself onto it heading south into black desert. He lacked the free will to turn around. His choices seemed just two—follow the washboard road or be guided by signs that led to Vegas. How many bad hunches had he followed before? The road led over a rise. Dust swirled over the windshield as he hit the brake on the downside of an arroyo.

He threw open the door and stepped out. The headlights aimed downhill. Golden eyes flickered in the beam, a fox or a coyote. He stepped away from the car to urinate. His breathing slowed as he listened to the splash of water on the hardpan. Finished, he zipped his trousers and looked at the sky. It was brilliant with stars, a blanket with billions of little holes letting spots of light through. He'd bet there were a trillion stars. Hell, he thought, I'd bet on the temperature of ice. He closed his eyes.

The car's engine idled roughly. He opened his eyes and walked back, reached in to turn off the lights, then the engine, and sat on the edge of the seat and looked about. Maybe, he thought, it was time to rid himself of hunches, find another plan. This seemed like a good spot. No one would find him for days. He opened the trunk and dug through sheets and towels until he found the valise. His fingers trembling, he unzipped it. The .32 was in the bottom where he'd packed it. It was small in his hand, seemed harmless. He held it out and felt the weight, then went to the front of the car, leaned against the fender, and released the safety. How would it feel? Would he suffer an instant of pain before death? And what if he bungled it? What if it didn't work? He wasn't going to take a chance—he aimed the gun skyward and pulled the trigger. The recoil was slight, but a two-foot tongue of flame spit out of the barrel. He wondered if it was better to place the barrel to his head or in his mouth. He decided on the temple, but as he touched the gun to his skin, it burned him and he jerked it away. It went off. Flame shot before his eyes. Powder stung his cheek and the tip of his nose.

It had deafened his right ear and his cheek and nose stung, but he was otherwise intact and unharmed.

Somewhere up the road a coyote made a choking sound. It seemed like laughter. Luther slumped against the fender, let his gun arm go limp, and wiped his eyes with his cuff. Luck. He heard the sound of the animal again and laughed at himself, an uncontrolled, deranged laugh swallowed by the open space. Then he stood upright and heaved the gun as far as he could into the desert. It hit something solid, a rock perhaps.

As he backed up and turned the car around, he felt the tables had already turned for him.

The fuel gauge read empty as he pulled into the Sands, where he gave the keys to the valet. He circled the blackjack pit searching for a dealer with a name tag reading "Don." After three trips, he paused at a dead game where a dour-faced dealer stood with his palms on the layout, trying his best to pretend Luther didn't exist. Luther asked if Don was working.

"Got a Dawn," the dealer said. "She's on roulette."

"No, a guy."

"Maybe graveyard shift."

Luther scanned the pit, but didn't see anything inviting him. All he had was a feeling, the name Don, seventy-two dollars, and strings of numbers parading through his mind. He looked at the dealer's name tag.

"Art, let's make some money," he said, dropping seventy in bills on the layout.

The dealer nodded. "I like what I hear so far," he said and called out "Shuffle" as he neatly divided the six decks into two even stacks.

Nothing too surprising happened in the next twenty minutes. Luther tripled his money and tipped Art about fifty dollars. Several dealers formed a line by the pit podium, and a pit boss sent them to games. Luther asked if Art was going on a break.

"Maybe. I've been in forty."

A second later a woman dealer stepped up behind Art, who turned his head slightly toward her and said, "Give this guy the rack." He thanked Luther and scooped up his tokes from behind the discard rack.

Art noted the woman's name tag as she buried a card from the shoe. "Hello, Vickie. You may be the woman of my dreams."

Her makeup made her skin look orange in the artificial light. She smiled. "Could be. And you may be the player of mine."

They understood one another clearly. She wanted him to win and expected him to reward her.

"Let's start with this," he said and placed a hundred and fifty in chips in the square and two five-dollar chips on the line in front for her.

"Okay. Good luck," she said.

She turned over a nine on his hand, took her up card, and gave him a two as a second card. She slipped her down card under and opened her up card—a six.

"Vickie, let's double down," he said and placed his last two five-dollar chips beside her bet. He had no cash to cover the call bet and no credit line. If he lost, he'd have to dash for the door before security could grab him. Then he remembered his car was in valet parking. Although his heart pounded like a distance runner's, he smiled and said calmly, "Mark the one fifty."

"Mark one fifty!" she called to the nearest pit boss, who routinely looked over and repeated the amount.

She gave him his double-down card—a deuce. She flipped her hole card over. It was a five to go with the six. Luther swallowed. Though his insides burned, he showed no emotion. She hit her hand with a deuce, then a three. Luther licked his lips. She turned an eight of clubs, which she laid softly and neatly by the other cards.

"Over," she said.

Though his insides were in turmoil, every muscle in Luther's face relaxed, as did his hands. The signs had been right all along.

He bet two hundred and caught a blackjack. The next hand was twenty, and he had three hundred in the square. Three hands after that he was firing a thousand at the house. He had no other thoughts, no memories by then, just his breathing and his heartbeat and each coming hand as the last one disappeared into the discard rack and died before it became a memory. This was existence as raw as that of any primitive beast in a jungle.

The next time he was aware of anything other than his cards and the wager in the box, a pit boss and a security guard were on either side of Vickie. The guard set a fill tray on top of the table. Three thousand in twenty-five-dollar chips and ten thousand in black chips. The pit boss extended his hand to Luther.

"Name's George," the boss said. "Yours?"

"Thomas," Luther said, desiring to keep his anonymity. And when the boss seemed to be waiting for more, he added the first surname that came to mind. "Thomas Pynchon."

"The writer?" the boss asked.

Jesus, Luther thought, I get the one pit boss in Vegas who's read a book and it happens to be by Thomas Pynchon. Nobody actually reads Thomas Pynchon. "Just coincidence," he said.

"Well, good luck."

Vickie signed her name to the fill slip and stuffed it in the drop box. Luther looked at the limit sign, stacked up his black chips and pushed them into the square.

"Chips play to the limit!" Vickie called out.

Luther caught a twenty. She turned up nineteen. For the next fifteen minutes that was the pattern the cards followed. By then two bosses were watching the play. Vickie seemed undaunted by it all. Luther had tipped her more than a thousand dollars and had her up on every bet for fifty more. He upped that to one hundred. She dealt him a four and six and gave herself a five for an up card. Luther doubled down his bet and placed another hundred beside her bet. The boss rushed over and pushed the second hundred back.

"One-hundred-dollar maximum for the dealer on a bet, Mr. Pynchon," he said.

Luther nodded. Vickie hit her hand to an eighteen and turned over Luther's card. He'd caught a nine. She paid the bets and thanked him as she picked up her tip. Luther looked at the boss.

"Can I do this?" he asked and set five black chips on the layout in front of Vickie. "For the dealer."

"It's your money," the boss said.

"I love it when they sweat," Luther said to Vickie.

A man swung into the third-base seat. "Looks like you're doing good here, pal," the man said as he laid a single green check in the player's square. "Think I'll give it go."

Luther nodded to him and said, "You're from New York."

"What gave it up, pal, the accent or the attitude?" The man laughed as if he had told a joke.

The dealer started to deal, but Luther withdrew his bet and held his palm up for her to stop. He looked at the New Yorker as he spoke to the dealer. "Call the boss over."

The pit boss came over, sullen-faced but congenial. "What's the problem, Mr. Pynchon?"

"Can you make this a reserved table?"

The pit boss shook his head. "Sorry, only the casino manager can do that, and he's not in the house."

The intruder smiled. "I don't see no problem," he said. "No one heard? It's unlucky to be superstitious. Besides, my money's as good as his."

Luther looked at the New Yorker as he addressed the pit boss. "Can you make it a five-hundred-dollar minimum?"

"Anything you want, Mr. Pynchon. Sorry," the pit boss said to the other man and removed the $25 MINIMUM sign.

The interloper scooped up his green check and stormed off, muttering as he did.

"People," Luther said to the dealer.

The dealer nodded.

In the next hour three new dealers were sent to deal to him. Luther won more than he lost, but something didn't sit well. He had a feeling that the run was over, that the man from New York had killed it. But something more was in operation. Where had the anticipation, the sudden constriction and expansion of the arteries, the adrenaline high gone? He remembered the feel of the hot barrel against his cheek, thought how that instant of unexpected pain had saved him and led to this moment. For what? The need to run was gone. He felt fatigued, as if he'd survived an ordeal—not as if he'd experienced something miraculous.

He stared at the mound of chips on the green felt layout. Without counting them down, he estimated his take at sixty-five thousand, enough to pay off Hy and plenty left over. He thought of asking for a room and calling Celeste. As he often did when thinking of her, he pictured her reaching out of the shower for a bath towel. Who knows? She might come. Would that be asking too much too soon?

He stood and raised his hand to signal he was quitting. "I'm going to get some rest," he said to the pit boss and asked for chip racks to carry his winnings to the cashier.

"I'd quit too," the dealer whispered as he took the cards out of the shoe and fanned them across the layout in symmetrically opposite semicircles.

Luther looked toward the edge of the pit, where a long line of dealers waited by the podium. He turned to the dealer behind the table. "Shift change?" he asked.

"Yeah, graveyard. I'm going home. You made our night. Thanks."

The pit boss was slow bringing the chip racks. When he did, he said that was a lot of money and asked if Luther wanted an escort to his car. Just as Luther was about to answer, he looked up at the graveyard dealer, a tall, thin man in his fifties with sleep-hungry eyes, salt-and-pepper hair, and the facial expression of a dog that had just been kicked. His name was Don.

Luther glanced from the $500 MINIMUM sign to the checks he'd placed in the rack. Acid churned in his stomach. Every bit of good sense told him to leave, to run, to hide from what he was about to do. He felt the hard constriction of his arteries and shrugged. He slumped in the chair, took out a stack of black checks, and said, "Shuffle up."

Don nodded. "Good luck, sir."

It hadn't taken long. An hour and a half. Luther shoved his way through the revolving door and entered the predawn light. The Strip glowed in an eerie way this time of morning when the sun was just a suggestion but enough of one that the artificial lights looked ghostlike. The valet greeted Luther and asked if he was picking up a car. Luther didn't seem to understand, so the parking attendant repeated himself. Luther shook his head, reached in his pockets, and felt around. He found two dollars. For an instant, he thought about how far he could get on two dollars' worth of gas and the rolls of quarters in the glove box, then he handed the bills to the valet.

"What's this for, sir?"

"You. For you," Luther said as he stepped away.

He walked the incline of the Flamingo overpass without looking back. There was no need. He recalled the hot wire on that fence many years before. He remembered singeing his palms and staring as welts rose on the soft white flesh. He couldn't explain the burns to his mother, except to say he'd had an accident. He'd gone back several times after to stare at the fence, but he'd never again touched it, for he understood its function.

Heading south, he ambled on numbly for a long stretch, and before he was aware of it, he was on the shoulder of Interstate 15 and the sun was high. The day was clear, a kind of bold day that called attention to itself. He took air deeply into his lungs. It smelled of exhaust fumes but seemed nonetheless invigorating, and he realized that only two hours before he'd felt fatigued. He smiled. He felt strangely unburdened. With an easy motion, he turned toward the oncoming traffic and held his shoulders back as he slowly extended his arm perpendicular to his body, his thumb raised high. He wondered how far a thumb and a smile would take him. Nothing else seemed important.

The God Gambler

FELICIA CAMPBELL

Of all the bizarros I've met in thirty years in Las Vegas, Roy Stuart was the bizarrest. There wasn't much to like about him. Marcy, his third wife, called him Rotten Roy, or Rotten for short. When she did, he'd just smile that sneaky little smile of his, because he was kind of proud of the name.

I met Roy in the fifties, before he started wearing sweatshirts with JESUS SAVES on the front and a picture of the crucifixion on the back. In those days life in Vegas was a twenty-four-hour party. We were craps dealers at the old Shangri La, one of the best Mob-run joints in the world. The big corporations hadn't moved in to turn us into bank clerks yet. We could rough-hustle for tokes and had a hell of a lot better chance of winning than the players did. When the shift was over, we'd grab our money and head next door to drop it at the nearest table.

Roy didn't seem too much different from anybody else in those days. Oh, he gambled and partied and talked loud with the rest of us, but nobody paid much attention to what he was saying, or that he always talked about himself. "I and another guy," he would begin. Every sentence started with "I" no matter how many people were involved. He wanted only two things out of life—to beat a craps table and to be married to a smart woman who would take care of him while he did it. It was his luck to get both.

By the mid-sixties, the party was just about over. The town was getting big, and management types, not gamblers, were running the clubs. Most of us were married or divorced, and either way had kids to think about, so we got serious about work. We had grown up and sobered up.

All but Roy. Oh, he got married and divorced a couple of times, to nice women too, and he had kids. Of course, he didn't worry about any of them; he knew their mothers would make do, so he stiffed them all on child support and kept playing.

When he married Marcy, he figured he had it made. She was new in town, had a good job, and looked like she was on her way up. None of us could figure out what she saw in him. Afterward, neither could she. She used to say that she had fallen for a pretty face, that about halfway through the wedding ceremony, she had known she was making a mistake, but it was ten years before women's lib and she didn't have the savvy to walk out.

On the drive to Tahoe for their honeymoon, he guzzled beer, threw the cans out the car window, and began to talk. Really talk. "I and another kid . . ." He battered her with "I's" until she couldn't believe that she had really married him. She stayed with him, though, for eleven years.

The bizarro part didn't start until she dumped him. He was in a real swivet with no one to take care of him. Then he met twenty-year-old Darla, and she fell for him. She was one nasty little broad, but she loved her daddy-husband, and Roy was saved in more ways than one. She belonged to a new cult that spoke in tongues and worshiped the Virgin Mary. As far as Darla was concerned, people who didn't belong weren't worth spitting on.

Of course Roy got "saved." When I met him to see if I could get him to pay Marcy's back child support, the first thing he told me was how the Virgin Mary kept appearing to him and telling him how to live his life. It was, "I and the Virgin Mary . . ."

He said that She had gotten him to quit drinking, which I had to admit was an improvement. She had also told him not to pay any more child support because Marcy and the kids were demon-possessed, which was why they wore sunglasses. So you couldn't see the devil looking out of their eyes. That was more than I could handle, so I left.

His buddy, Saul, a girlie photographer, who was as close as Roy came to having a friend, told me the rest of the story.

According to Saul, the Virgin finally got down to business around Christmastime, when She told Roy that he should gamble for the Lord. His church needed money for a new roof and trees, and Roy had it at his command to satisfy those wants. Just before She had appeared this time, Roy had watched *The Little Drummer Boy* on television, and this fit right in.

As soon as She faded, he put on his baby-blue sweatshirt with

PRAISE THE LORD on the front, and a picture of Mary at Lourdes on the back, got into his pickup truck, and headed for Circus Circus.

When he got there, he didn't even bother to look up at the Flying Caverettas performing over his head but made a beeline for the middle craps table, where he knew one of the balloon-shirted dealers. In two hours he was wiped out and drag-assed himself home to think it over.

There was nothing he could do but wait until the Virgin showed up again to tell him what he had done wrong. When She did, She told him to convert those around him while he was playing. This way, he could win money for the church and save souls at the same time.

He told Darla, and she fell right in with it, never doubting him for a minute, and decided to go along.

They put on their matching black sweatshirts with JESUS SAVES on the front and the crucifixion on the back and went to Caesars Palace. When they walked through the casino—Roy's pop eyes half shut under his Greek sailor's hat and Darla radiating pea-green nastiness, mouth sneering over her big teeth, her long black hair stringing over the crucifixion till you could only see the feet—people gave way in disbelief.

Roy forced his way in at a table with heavy action. Darla, trying to follow, kept getting in the players' way. When someone would ask her to move, she would refuse, adding, "God bless you," which really pissed off a lot of people. The boxman finally raised an eyebrow to the floorman, who touched her arm and asked her to move away from the table if she didn't intend to bet. Stringy hair flying, she whipped around, almost upsetting one of Caesar's handmaidens carrying a full tray of drinks, and shrieked, "Fucker" at the floorman for putting his hand on her. He motioned a security guard, who escorted her outside and told her not to come back in.

By now Roy was on a roll. Jumping up and down, throwing the dice and praising the Lord at the top of his lungs, he exhorted his fellow gamblers to follow his lead and never missed Darla for a second.

People from all over the casino crowded around to watch the sideshow. Security stayed close, watching both Roy and the crowd, but things stayed cool.

It was Roy's big moment. He wasn't a bully, or a drunk, or a wastrel, or even the Little Drummer Boy. He was, by God, a crusader, and *he was beating a craps table.*

Meanwhile Darla had gone around to the side entrance and was making her way back in past Cleopatra's Barge to stand by her man, the last thing Roy, who had completely forgotten her existence, needed.

He was up to twenty-one straight passes, and the Lord was with him. His heart pounded and the veins stood out on his forehead over his pop eyes, as he made the twenty-second straight pass. The crowd held its breath. Half of them wanted him to win, and the other half wanted to watch him drop dead when he couldn't hack the stress.

By the time Darla reached the area, he was up to twenty-four straight passes, and there was one hell of a lot of chips in front of him.

She pushed and shoved and God blessed and praised the Lord at that crowd until they saw by her shirt that she was his old lady and let her through. The floorman shook his head at security, motioning them not to move on her. She got to the side of the table just as Roy made his twenty-sixth straight pass.

He had the dice in his hand for the twenty-seventh glorious roll, when Darla, the woman he had married to care for him and save him from care, screamed, *"Roy! Quit! That's enough!"*

His face crumpled as he dropped the dice. He made a half-hearted gesture to pull in his chips, and, for the first time in his adult life, he started to cry.

Darla was real proud of herself. The crowd hated her, but they moved so she could get to Roy's side.

When she got there, Roy made his twenty-seventh straight pass, right under her chin. He hit her so hard, he lifted her right up in the air and landed her, snake eyes, on the table—JESUS SAVES side up.

Las Vegas Courtship

ROBERT DODGE

I used to listen to Jimmy Reeves sing about "out where the bright lights are shining," and I'd think, "God damn, he must have been to Octavius." I knew the feeling; I wanted to get out of the four walls, out of the dark and into the bright lights. I made up my mind that as soon as I could, I'd find the brightest lights in the world and I'd settle down where I could see them every night. Not really much of an ambition now I look back on it, but I guess I made it.

That's how I came to live in Las Vegas, though it didn't have to be Las Vegas. It could have been Syracuse or Binghamton or New York City, but all of those places were too close to Octavius. Besides, there was something special about Las Vegas. A sense of adventure that even Chicago and New York couldn't conjure up for me. Partly it came from the gambling, partly the West and the desert, and partly the lights.

I think I felt a kind of historical sense, too. My great-great-grandfather had gone west as one of the original miners in both California and Nevada. He'd panned for gold on the Stanislaus, and he'd worked for wages in the Comstock. He even struck it rich once, but he sold out for a hundred thousand dollars and invested it all in mining stocks. He should have known as much about stocks as he did about mines. Father used to say that the law of averages should at least have hit him one good share, but it didn't. Father and I burned the stocks after Grampa died. Grampa hung on to the idea that one day they'd make us all rich. I guess that's what his grandfather used to tell him. Father and I threw a whole bushel basket full into the fireplace. When the last one had blackened and shriveled into gray powder, Father said, "One man's dreams are as good as another's. 'Dust to dust, ashes to ashes.' It's all the same in the end."

Grampa had always wanted to travel west, to see the places his grandfather had gone. He never did, though. He'd keep saying, "Yes, sir, next year I'm going out to California," but it was always next year. I don't think he ever got west of Buffalo.

Instead, he used to tell stories about his grandfather. Father never cared for the stories, never cared about the dreams, but I used to listen to them all the time. By the time I was four, I asked for them by name. "Tell me about great-great-grandfather and the Indians. Tell me about the Mormons. Tell me how your Grampa struck it rich." Grampa used to tell them. I grew to believe in a Wild West filled with adventure and excitement. Like Grampa, I kept promising myself that next year I'd go have a look at it. I'd compare the West that Grampa talked about to Octavius and know I had to go.

So, when Father died, about a year after Mother, I sold the house and farm; I paid off the mortgage and took ten thousand dollars to Las Vegas. For the first two weeks, I stayed at Caesars Palace, screwed a different whore every night and gambled a lot. The people at Caesars knew I had ten thousand in one of their boxes and they treated me like a man with ten thousand dollars to lose. At the end of two weeks I counted my money. I had fifteen dollars more than I'd had when I left Octavius. I thought I had the system figured out.

I guess I made a mistake counting my money. I know that as soon as I did, I started to lose. Las Vegas lost its shine. The whores seemed hard. The luxury of the hotel turned to plastic. It scared me to gamble, but it scared me not to gamble. Somewhere a long run would come up. I knew it. It lay there waiting in the dice. I feared that I might miss it. I even hated to go to the bathroom. I'd hold it as long as I could and then rush off and rush back to the table, worried that someone might have won big while I urinated.

Once an old man came up to the table, watched the dice for a few rolls, and then placed a hundred-dollar chip on the nine. He won. Jokingly, I turned and asked him how he'd known. He told me. Like half the craps players in Vegas, he had a system and was convinced that it worked. I'd seen enough: I knew it worked, too. Hadn't I seen it with my own eyes? For the next two or three days, I don't know which, I followed him all over the Strip. He acted as if he didn't need sleep, and so did I. He didn't mind my tagging along. During those days I forgot about whores; I forgot about Octavius; I forgot about the time of day. The bright lights were shining for me. I'd seen the answer; the way to wealth shone clearly ahead of us.

Later the only thing I could see clearly was that the old man's system didn't work. None of them do. I had three thousand left. The old man had less. He blamed me. "You're a jinx, son. Get away."

When I got back to my room, I found that my bags had been checked and the room had been rented to tourists from Nebraska. I got my bags at the desk and moved to a cheaper hotel. For the next two weeks, I moved from cheap hotel to cheaper hotel. Finally I ended up at the Desert Sage Motel in North Las Vegas. I had lost all but about five hundred dollars.

For the next two months I lived at the Desert Sage. A typical cheap motel, it had all the usual signs in the lobby as well as some I'd never seen before. NO PETS. YOUR LUGGAGE MAY NOT BE RE-MOVED FROM YOUR ROOM UNTIL YOUR BILL HAS BEEN SETTLED. UNREGISTERED GUESTS, TEN DOLLARS EXTRA. SOME MONEY IS BETTER THAN NO MONEY, MAKE US AN OFFER.

I made them an offer. Five dollars a day. The clerk said forty dollars a week, and I took it. From the Desert Sage I could walk to the cheaper North Las Vegas casinos, casinos where I could get a bet down for fifty cents, sometimes even twenty-five. I still knew that there had to be a run for me. All I had to do was hold on until my lucky run came up. I'd make back all the money I had lost and more. I could do it in North Las Vegas just as quickly as in Caesars Palace.

I went on to other games. If it was a matter of luck, maybe my luck would improve at keno or roulette or twenty-one. At keno I picked eight numbers and stuck with them. I had a chance to win twenty-five thousand dollars for sixty cents. I knew that those eight numbers would come up. I had to have my money down when they did.

And they did come up once. Just as I walked into the casino I looked up at the keno board, and my eight numbers blinked back at me. "We thought you were here. You should have come five minutes earlier. You slept too late. You lingered too long over the forty-nine-cent breakfast. You missed your big chance."

"Wait, wait."

They blinked back at me. "Too late. Too late."

I started playing the slot machines. I knew a jackpot waited in them. Maybe the next nickel would get it. Maybe the next one. I was afraid to put money in them, but I was even more afraid of missing that one big jackpot that would start me back on the road to riches.

I had reached my last two hundred dollars when Ruth asked me to buy her breakfast. She'd been living on free hot dogs and forty-nine-cent breakfasts for the last week and a half. Poor Ruth. She'd thought it would be easy to get a job in Las Vegas. She didn't know the right places to look. She'd just left Johnson City, Iowa, and her first four applications had been turned down simply because the jobs had already been filled, but that had been enough to discourage her. Now she had no more money. She was thinking of wiring her father for money to come home.

I got it all out of her at breakfast. She told me that I was the seventh person she'd asked for breakfast and the first who had simply said yes.

"The women and families just look at you as if you're dirt. The men either hurry by and don't see you, or else they say, 'Sure, come on over to my motel, and I'll have room service send up a big platter of steak and eggs.' You're the only person who just said, 'Sure.' How come?"

"I don't know. Why not? It's only forty-nine cents."

"Well, that's what you would think, isn't it? After all, it's not that much money. Not unless you don't have it, but, I don't know, it seems like nobody wants to buy you breakfast in this town."

"I know. I think they're all afraid."

"Afraid?"

"Of being taken."

"You think so?"

"Sure, maybe they're all afraid you don't really need the money. That after you eat the breakfast you'll go away and laugh at them. You read about stuff like that in the paper. Bigger stuff, but the same sort of thing. So, to guard against it, they get real careful on the small stuff. Me? I don't care. Maybe you've got a thousand dollars in your pocketbook. That's all right. I'll buy you a breakfast because I like you, even if you don't need it."

By this time she had finished her eggs and sausage. She wiped up the last driblets of yolk with a piece of toast, saw that I had noticed and blushed. "Excuse my manners. I just don't want to let any of it go to waste."

"I don't blame you. In fact I was about to say that I like you so much I'll buy you a dinner if you want to come with me."

Her eyes fixed on me. "What do you want?"

"Just because I like you. And maybe I do want something. You know you're the first person I've talked to in a month?"

She looked shocked. I believe she thought I was crazy. "Really?"

"No, not really. I mean, I've said things like 'Give me some more chips' and 'How much is this room?' but I haven't talked to anyone. You made me realize it. Come on, let me buy you a dinner. I like to talk to you."

We went to another North Las Vegas casino. Here the special attraction was a steak dinner for a dollar ninety-five. I ordered one for each of us.

She told me about the town she had come from. To me it sounded a lot like Octavius except for the hills and trees. Johnson City, Iowa. The kids in her high school used to call it the asshole of the universe.

"That's what they called Octavius, too."

"Really? It seems like everybody wants to get out of the place where he is."

"Doesn't it?"

I told her how I used to listen to Jimmy singing "Four Walls." How I used to dream about the bright lights.

"I know what you mean. I had to get out of Johnson City. I just had to. Everybody was after me."

"After you?"

"To do what they thought I ought to do. 'Go to college, get married, have kids, get a job.' You know. Nobody thought dancing was worth anything."

"You're a dancer?"

"I thought I was until I came here."

"Thought you were?"

"If I was really a dancer, I'd get a job, wouldn't I?"

"Maybe, maybe not. The way I figure it is you're either a dancer or you're not. If you're a dancer, you dance because you like to dance, because you have to make that beauty with your body. To hell with the job."

"But I've got to have a job. I've got to live."

"I knew a man back in Octavius. Everybody thought he was crazy. The only jobs he ever got were patching roofs, sweeping out bars, that kind of thing."

"So?"

"So they thought he was crazy because he liked to paint. He was an artist. He died, and his kids burned up all his paintings because they thought he was crazy, too, and they didn't want the paintings around to remind them of their crazy father, but he was still an artist."

"I'll tell you a secret."

"Okay."

"I tried to get a job over across the street. That's where I was last night."

"At the strip joint?"

"Yes. They said I could be in the amateur dance contest. Maybe I could win a hundred dollars, and I went out and I really danced for them. Then I heard them yelling, 'Take it off, take it off, take it off.' I took my skirt off and they cheered; I took my blouse off, and they cheered louder. Well, I thought, it's really no different than dancing in leotards, but still they kept yelling, 'Take it off, take it off,' and I looked down on them. I took off my bra. I kind of enjoyed dancing without my bra. I'd done it before in my bedroom, and they kept yelling and yelling, and when I didn't take off my panties, somebody started to boo. I even started to take them off, but then the music stopped and I ran off the stage. I didn't win anything. They didn't even ask me to come back and try again."

"I don't blame you," I said.

"Well, I don't either, but I've got to do something. I spent my last fifteen cents for a cup of coffee this morning. I've got exactly three pennies in my purse. That's it. What can I buy for three pennies? I don't even like bubble gum." She laughed. "Maybe I should go back there tonight and take everything off. Maybe I should call my father."

"Have you had enough to eat?" I asked.

She looked at me. "Yes, I have. Thank you. I didn't mean to bore you with my problems."

"That's all right. I'm not bored. I just want to take them one at a time."

"Well, yes, then. I've had enough to eat. I can't remember the last time I had a full belly."

"Where have you been sleeping?"

"At the bus station. Yeah, I go down to the bus station and pretend I'm waiting for a bus. I've done that three nights now, but last night they told me to get out unless I had a ticket."

"Are you tired?"

She yawned, as if I'd reminded her. "Yes, of course, I'm tired. I don't know. I guess I'll call my father. It's either that or find some man to live with until I get a job. God knows, I've had plenty of those offers."

"Is that what you want to do?"

"No, it's not. Well, I wouldn't care, you know, if I liked somebody and didn't have to. But everyone just assumes that since I'm broke I'll jump at the chance to be a mistress. It's all so economic."

"I still think we should take things one at a time. You're tired, you need sleep. Here's the key to my motel room. Put up the DO NOT DISTURB sign. I won't bother you."

"Really?"

"Really. Tell you what. I'll meet you here at six o'clock tonight; I'll buy you another dinner and give you a dime to call your father if that's what you want to do."

"Thank you. I'll see you at six." She got up to leave. A minute later she was back. "I forgot to ask. How do you get to your motel?"

I told her. She leaned over and kissed me on the lips. Very briefly, but still a kiss. "You're awfully nice."

"That's okay. It doesn't cost me anything."

"But that's not how most of them look at it; they look at what they can get out of it. They think they've lost something unless they get the most they can out of any situation."

She left and I went back to the tables, but I couldn't seem to get interested in gambling. I kept thinking about Ruth. The numbers didn't talk to me anymore. Somehow I knew that the jackpot wouldn't come up with the next pull of the handle, that the next roll of the dice wouldn't start a run. I actually won twenty dollars that day. I figured it out that I'd earned three dollars an hour. Not much better than farming.

Maybe that's what stopped me that time. If I'd kept losing I probably wouldn't have stopped until it was all gone. Compulsive gamblers hardly ever do. That's what they tell us, anyway, but this time I stopped.

It wasn't just the three dollars an hour. Ruth had a lot to do with it. I wanted to see her again. I wondered if she would meet me. I knew there were women in town who made a business of stealing men's luggage.

But not Ruth. She met me at the same restaurant. We ate supper; we talked; we drank some wine. I found out that her father was a dairy farmer, too; we talked about cows for half an hour. She and her father were Ayrshire people. My father, like almost all the dairy-men in New York, had raised Holsteins. The one thing that neither of us liked about Ayrshires or Holsteins was cleaning up after them. Cows make shit; there's no getting around that. If I was a breeder, I'd try to develop a shitless cow. People laugh when they hear that. Ruth laughed, too, but she had to admit it was a good idea. After all, they made a seedless orange; that sounds even more impossible than a shitless cow.

That was just one of the things Ruth and I talked about that night. I'd never talked silly like that with a woman before. How many women are there in the world that you could talk about cow manure with? Not very many, I bet. I never tried it with anyone but Ruth.

I'd had a wild idea ever since I met Ruth that morning. After we ate, I told her about it. It took awhile to work up to it.

"You know, I've lost almost ten thousand dollars in the last month."

"That's a lot of money. I guess some people can afford it."

"I guess some people can."

"Meaning you can't."

"Right. I've got two hundred and seven dollars left."

"Oh, gee. That's too bad." She waited a minute. "Was it fun?"

"You know something? I hadn't even thought about whether it was fun. No, I guess it wasn't. No, I guess it was desperate. Terrible."

"I'm sorry."

"What can you do? The money's gone. Today I quit gambling. Thanks to you."

"Me?"

"Right. Just talking to somebody. Just getting my mind off the craps tables and the keno numbers. I think it stopped me. You helped me save two hundred dollars. I want to give you half of it."

"Why?"

"Why not? I like you. I would have lost it anyway if I hadn't met you. This'll give you a chance to get a job, stick around for a while, make up your mind."

"I can't take it."

"Sure you can. You can pay me back sometime if you want to, but you don't have to."

"I wouldn't take it if I didn't need it."

"I know." I handed her a folded hundred-dollar bill. "I know you can't last long on that. I hope you find something soon."

"I will. I bet I can get a job as a waitress or something. You're right. I don't have to get paid for it to be a dancer." She looked at me—soft brown eyes, a bit of a smile. I felt my stomach turn. "You know what I said about living with a man?"

"Sure."

"I think I'd like to live with you."

Bowling with the Christ Child

DAYVID FIGLER

I'm bowling with the Christ Child at the Orleans Hotel and Casino in Las Vegas, Nevada. We've got a lane to ourselves. Pretty cool, right, but I'm slightly embarrassed because we have to have the bumpers up so the ball doesn't roll into the gutter. Yeah, it's Christ, but He's still a child. I want to be encouraging. Build confidence. Odd thing is, even with the bumpers, the Christ Child is bowling a really lousy game. He sort of struggles up there with the eight-pounder, stops cold, and hauls it down the lane. The ball hits the bumper, rides the rail until it knocks down one, maybe two pins.

"Good job, Jesus, woo, you got a few—all right!"

Now I'm no Dick Weber or Mark Roth, but I am putting the young Savior to shame. Bowling is very important, even in my dreams, and I'm capable of reaching the ever-elusive 200 for the first time. Meanwhile, the Christ Child is carrying something like a 12 in the seventh frame. When I'm up, the Christ Child hits the button that illuminates the red Brunswick crown on the score projector, which in turn calls over the cocktail waitress. Upon returning to the scoring table each frame, she's there again.

And Jesus says, "He'll have the nachos."

But I don't want the nachos. I explain to the Christ Child that I have a very sensitive stomach. He tells her to add extra jalapeños.

He says, ". . . by eating the jalapeños, you will become closer to G-d."

I acquiesce. On her next trip, I order a Coke. When she brings it I taste, and frown, because it's a Diet Coke. I'm about to call her back and the Christ Child says, "I did that. I just learned how."

"Great!" I say, not looking forward to the bitter aftertaste of Diet Coke, but of course I have to drink it now because it's *His* miracle.

In the eighth frame, He's talking to some bowlers in the next alley. One is a salesman tossing back Jägermeister out of an eight-ounce plastic cup. Like purple-tinged NyQuil being shotgunned from a cap that's way too big for the dosage. It's still afternoon. He looks like Sean Penn with an oily mustache. His wife, also bowling, is six inches taller than him. Blond hair and lots of freckles on her deeply tanned breasts, which are very apparent. The salesman is helping the Christ Child assemble a little tiny cross from a kit. They put one training wheel underneath it, and both seem pleased with the final product.

"Jesus," I say, "you're up."

The Christ Child returns to the lane and puts His hand over the air blower thing. He leaves it there—for a maddeningly long time. And His hand just stays there.

"Does that help you?" I ask.

He thinks for a minute and turns His head back to me. "It doesn't help anyone, but it helps everyone." With that He takes the ball and knocks down one pin.

The bowlers in the next alley wave good-bye to us and giggle their way back to the front desk to return their rental shoes. I notice they had no trouble with the knots in the laces. Another Christ Child intervention.

"My Mother keeps a diary of everything I do," the Christ Child says. "First tooth, first crawl, first time I stand without help, first words. She writes things in great detail—each day is about forty pages long. Each volume is beautifully bound in faux leather and includes a forward from Doctor Spock about the challenges of child rearing and the horrors of war. People want to make Her writings into the new new testament, but since they would never fit into a motel room bureau drawer, they will forever go unpublished."

Great. Where's his Mother now that I'm in the action? I think to myself. I say, "Interesting. Do you think I'll make it in there?"

"Oh, yes, most definitely, you will. But don't forget your mother has such a book, too." With that He asked me to hand Him the bag of samples that the salesman had given Him. It was filled with oils and resins and things. "Bowling sacraments," He says as He begins to apply them to His hands and bowling ball. He says, "We are all Christ."

"So was my mother right when she said that I'm the Messiah?"

"Yes, we are all anointed."

"And to think I got mad at Mom for jacking my expectations way too high. I stiffed her on Mother's Day."

"You did not honor your mother and for that you were tormented."

"Some time later, the guilt became maddening."

"Like the air from the air blower thing?" He suggests before picking up His ball, rolling and hitting three pins.

I don't buy His words, and half jokingly respond, "I once thought I had stigmata, but it turned out to be a leaky burrito supreme."

"That," He said, "was no accident, and the unearthly flickering glow at the Taco Bell that you attributed to faulty wiring in the fluorescent lights above was also part of the sign."

"Okay . . ." I offer, slowly.

"No, really, fast-food restaurants are the perfect place for the Creator to impress upon us that the sole purpose of life is to operate within the confines of His Word. Lack of nutrition, which causes abdominal discomfort, gives us pause to understand that the Garden is inside each of us; it needs constant tending. The further we stray from His Word, the more we are tormented. People may follow me, so long as they do not contradict His words. After all, I'm just a little kid bowling."

I finish my game. 199. He actually picks up a spare in the tenth, but then rolls a one.

"Always on my spare!" He laments.

His Mother appears, surrounded by angels in keno runner garb. She wears an elegant but simple deep blue pea coat with the tiniest Dukakis/Bentsen button on the lapel. "Let's go, honey. It's time for gymnastics." A gentle but firm address. Without hesitation He packs up. I am thanked for watching Him. I say he was a delight. She asks for the proper spelling of my name. The entourage all ascends upon a magical escalator that disappears into a misty Nirvana; perhaps it's the next themed property for the Strip to replicate. I fiddle with the knot in my rental shoes, the knot from the nachos, and take two fruit-flavored TUMS because I'm sure I have to.

When I wake up from this dream, I say to myself, "I should just buy a pair of bowling shoes. They'll pay for themselves soon enough." And it's true.

I bowl often when the world gets a little heavy. The moment I cherish the most is when I release the ball and know that it is about to glide perfectly into the sweet pocket for a solid hit. There is absolute silence before contact. I start to turn and thrust my clenched fist down in victory while my knee juts up to meet my elbow at my tummy and I exult, "Yes!"

Sometimes, when the dust has cleared, the ten pin stands.

The Funniest Thing
You Said All Night

ANDREW KIRALY

I was in my parents' kitchen with coffee and the JobLink classifieds when my night, as they say, went to shit. What happened was someone started ringing the doorbell and knocking like a Jehovah's Witness on Judgment Day. I opened the door and said, "What the he—? Oh, hi, officer." A squat, crew-cut cop with a rifle. Incident next door, he said. Have to evacuate your house. Get what you need and be outside in two minutes. But *stay on the porch.*

I told them. Dad grumbled from his recliner; Mom tittered. We went to the porch, and the cop "covered" us—training his rifle on the second-story window of Red's house next door—as we walked gingerly down the driveway to Dad's truck. The cop said it might be an hour or two until things were settled. He said we might want to get something to eat, or maybe catch a movie. How nice of him. Then he waved us away and said, "Let's move it!" As we turned off Edith Avenue, another cop stretched a line of yellow plastic tape from one street corner to the other.

We rode around for an hour, bouncing judgments off Red and his family, a backboard for our scruples: they had to be our neighbors, knew it would come to something like this—a gun?!—wondered how long it would be till they made it up in their Jacuzzi, etc. It was another tool to avoid conversation. See, my family's version of communication was asking where the remote was, what form of cow meat was for dinner. Think white noise. Think elevator music. And since I'd left home six months ago—now I was back, pretending to visit—it didn't exactly look like Mom and Dad had started a tear-welling series of squishy heart-to-hearts.

"I wave to him if he's out when I check the mail. I don't know why I do," Mom said. "I guess I still believe kindness can change people."

Dad said, "Don't even talk to them. They're animals. Period."

"They still get kinky in the Jacuzzi?"

"Jason," Mom said, "that's just vulgar."

"I always wondered if they used extra chlorine." I couldn't help it: my mouth was always working against me. Even tonight, when I least needed it to.

"Enough," Dad said. For a second I wondered whether my newly independent station in life nullified his authority to whack me upside the head. I doubted it.

"Sorry," I said.

Dad got on the freeway for no particular reason, got off, then drove downtown, stopped at a 7-Eleven to buy the same USA Today we had at home. Then as the sun set we drove around some more, vaguely circling our neighborhood, waiting for Phoenix's finest to finish using our yard as a sniper's nest. Dad grew sour and silent while Mom drifted from speculating what exactly Red Reese had done to talking about the Guinness Book of World Records. It had a category for just about everything, she said, including a record for the number of beer kegs (empty) balanced on someone's head.

Mom said, "One woman from Germany stacked fifty-two sofa cushions on her head. I read that book for two hours straight today. It's addictive. Help me!" She laughed. Mom had retired from nursing a year ago; now she spent most of her time doing jigsaw puzzles and reading Guinness.

"Is there a category for chihuahuas?"

"I doubt it."

"Colostomy bags?"

"Jason. That's vulgar."

Then I said, "Dad, are you ever going to speak again?"

"No."

Mom said, "He's grumpy because he's missing boxing. It was that Mexican gentleman you like so much, wasn't it? Cervantes?"

"Heh. Good one, Mom."

Dad just steered, sulking.

"When we get back home, let's see how many rolls of toilet paper we can balance on Dad's head," I said. I have never known how to make this man smile. This ploy was as good as any. Tonight, though, the stakes were higher than usual.

"He probably wouldn't notice. You know how he shuts off when he watches boxing. He's on a different planet. Aren't you, Joe?"

"Well, maybe they'll postpone the fight due to rain," I said. Not a peep from the guy, as usual. Par for the course.

"Earth to Joe. Your son just made a joke," Mom said.

"I heard, darling." His words were prickly with irony.

"See how he monopolizes the conversation?" I said.

Mom laughed. "You should use that."

"How the heck would I use that?"

"You could use that on the hagglers."

"Hecklers," Dad said.

"Is that what they're calling them these days?" Mom said and pinched my arm. Hagglers was an inside joke.

Dad was always ready to correct you. And if you weren't correctable, you were scratched off the list, considered lost. I was currently a card-carrying member of the latter group. He'd written me off when I moved away six months ago after one of those cataclysmic father-son blowups. I think I had said something along the lines of the sun turning into a neutron star before I set foot back into house. When you're invoking astronomical concepts like that, you know you're into some serious shit.

I said, "Mom is well aware that haggling is what people do in countries without supermarkets."

"Do you get many hagglers?"

"Why do you keep saying that?" Dad said.

"I don't get many regular audience members, let alone hagglers."

"Harder than you figured, isn't it?" Dad said. *Now* he was talking. And he sounded satisfied.

"Which only means it's worth the effort," I said, more curtly than I should have.

I'd left our happy home in Phoenix six months ago to break into stand-up comedy in Las Vegas. Sin City whupped my ass. So here I was, the Prodigal Son returned, though my parents didn't know it quite yet. They thought the Prodigal Son was just here to say hi and drink all their Cokes. Until I popped the question, anyway.

"People just need time to take a liking to you," Mom said. "I think you could do a whole show on what's happened tonight alone.

You've missed several things next door since you've been gone, you know. Maybe I'll start videotaping."

The truck jarred to a stop. Dad said to the red Mazda that had swooped in front of him, "Jesus Christ, use your signals!"

What had happened tonight was that Red Reese went berserk. Or something like that. The cop at our door hadn't told us much, just that Red was drunk and wielding a shotgun. Sure, I knew the Reese family was far from perfect. Red would often hibachi-barbecue ribs in his front yard, never failing to scorch a good portion of his yellow lawn. He regularly blasted Steppenwolf from his garage as he drank beer and performed obscure operations on his cobalt-blue Mustang. His friends came over weekends, shouted and drank and sometimes vomited on the row of azaleas separating our yards. His five-year-old daughter, Debbie, squatted to pee in the street when the mood struck her. And about once a week, Red and his wife, Judy, had an explosive fight—slamming doors, sobbing, screaming, his Mustang finally peeling out of the oil-stained driveway at some ungodly hour—a fight that always resulted in a cop or two pounding on their door. But nothing like guns had ever been involved. I didn't even know Red owned a gun. Exasperating as he was, Red had never quite seemed dangerous.

Even Red and Judy's fights seemed innocuous at bottom. They always made up in grand style. At the time I had faith that Red and Judy would sort even this one out, that Red would emerge from the standoff unscathed, triumphant, and he and Judy would celebrate with a splashy humpty-hump in the Jacuzzi. That's what they always did to make up after a row. When they'd get going in there on summer evenings, I swear, with our patio door open, we could hear them grunting and sighing and sloshing as if it were in our own living room: white trash Jacuzzi sex in Surround Sound! Then Dad would pick up the remote, the TV volume bar would go up, up, until the orchestrated mania of *Jeopardy* would make our walls vibrate and our ears practically bleed. Mom and Dad would do the uncomfy squirm-and-cough, which always made me say things like, "That reminds me—I ain't been laid in months!" The sole purpose being, of course, to offend them, zap them. Mostly Dad. I was always zapping him in those days before I left with two suitcases and a shitload of indignation, and in that sense Red was my unknowing coconspirator. He helped me zap Dad. Red and I had exchanged no more than five words in our entire lives, but as a figure of suburban roguery, he was my ally.

Now I needed to move back home. Now I was trying to undo things. I was antizapping, unzapping, dezapping. Trying to make Dad laugh, open up the door a crack. Think bucket and sponge at an Arctic Sea oil spill. Think unfolding an origami chandelier.

Dad turned toward home. No luck. Yellow police tape was still stretched across Edith Avenue; gawkers had begun to cluster on the street corners. So we continued driving nowhere, purposeless, this sudden, forced intimacy making my whole visit even more uncomfortable.

"Are you hungry, Joe?"

"No."

"I could eat a rhino," I said.

"We can stop somewhere," Mom said.

"I was speaking figuratively, of course. I'd hate to have to prove that."

Dad sighed.

"This man's life is in jeopardy. Get him a televised boxing match, quick," I said. Dad just stared ahead, his thoughts no doubt locked on visions of Molson Ice and boxing. What can you say to a man who in his life has laughed about as many times as he's worn a tux? "Mrs. Vesey, I'm sorry to inform you your husband has turned to stone."

"He might look nice in the garden."

He said, "All these jokes. You say these things onstage?"

Mom said, "Joe."

"I'm hurt," I said. "I saved my best material for you two. I haven't used these since I launched my illustrious standup career."

Launched. Ha ha ha. Rockets launch; porn stars launch; standup careers sputter and sometimes miraculously fall upward. But not in Vegas. Vegas is a place where standup comedy is about as popular as recreational spinal taps. The entertainment scene is a feudal system of high-concept boobs-and-lasers shows on one end and Velveeta lounge acts on the other. In my brief tenure, the few worthwhile showrooms that did feature any standup were still working on the old-school payola system. And my bank account—if not my dignity—precluded such a route. So I had scraped up a few open-mike gigs at off-the-Strip bars, making cracks to sparse crowds of hard-hat beer monkeys, grizzled alkies, and fraternity mooks. I won't lie: it sucked harder than a Hoover. Sure, I was a smart-ass—but a standup comedian? That's like the difference between being able to change your oil and being an auto mechanic. So now I was soaping up my brain with the idea of returning to school. But this time seriously. I swear. I was gravitating toward philosophy again. Hell, I'd already majored in it twice.

I'd left Phoenix on bad terms. First, I had dropped out of college for the second time, using the thin pretense of being troubled by some mysterious higher goal, like I was some restless visionary. I hung around the house in my socks, reading Hesse and Sartre and Hegel and pretending to get it; I wrote inscrutable, bad poetry. I smoked cloves in the garage. I gotta say this about philosophy; the stuff should *not* be sold over the counter. Reading philosophy has this way of hypersensitizing you to the glaring, contemptible mundaneness of the world, a category that includes most, if not all, facets of my parents' life as suburban retirees: that wait for death stultified with satellite television, Brachs candy, and leather recliners. Philosophy thus turned me into a smug asshole, looking down his nose at the packet of conventions that passes for living in the twenty-first century.

For instance, I would read some David Hume, then I'd go after Dad, asking him questions like, "If I drop this spoon, will it fall?"

"Yes, it will." He'd roll his eyes, just barely. Think brooding rhino. Think grumpy brontosaurus.

"No. You cannot say with certainty it will. You have merely based that so-called certainty on a string of past experiences which have happened to confirm your expectations."

"You're going to be miserable in that heat if you don't cut the grass soon."

This phase of dropout-turned-living-room-philosopher lasted about two weeks, during which time Dad said nothing. Now I realize he was giving me time to mend my ways. The ultimatum came down: go back to school, he said, or get a job and move out. He favored the former; he said he didn't care if I got some bullshit degree in philosophy, just get the degree. And let's face facts, he said, it *is* bullshit. But if you want to get paid to say black is white and white is black, go right ahead and get the degree. Even a degree like that would open up doors. And if I thought I could do without schooling, I'd better think hard. Because, son—he said *son* when he was serious about something—you're at a crossroads. He meant *crossroads* in the sense that I was choosing my now-or-never Ultimate Path, that this would determine the general trajectory of all my future life.

I didn't take kindly to his advice; anything but. In fact, I was ablaze with indignation: how dare this sofa wart—this retired machinist with merely a high school diploma—rush my calling, and in doing so disrupt its delicate transmission? He didn't understand; I needed time to study my map of possibilities and see what road magically shivered with my destiny. This TV-addled machinist didn't know *shit* about life—the real, inner life of dreams and true vocations, et cetera. In short, I wanted to show him. I took a rapid, sobbing inventory of my scant resources: I had always been a moderately clever wiseass; that, coupled with my white-hot desire to somehow thumb my nose at Dad, led me to Vegas. Yeah. I would be a standup comedian in the Entertainment Capital of the World. My blazing success would be giving him the finger on a whole new order. I'd be mashing his physical-labor-obsessed work ethic back into his face with a job that didn't require me—not literally, anyway—to lift a finger.

So I caught a Greyhound to Vegas. I had no connections, no plans, and very little material. But indignation has this way sometimes of steeling you with a sense of purpose, you know what I mean?

My first couple weeks "working" were open-mike nights at this place called Bead's Bar, a fairly presentable place that even had tablecloths. The guy in charge of comedy was a sweet, white-haired comedian named Louie whose career peak was opening up for Jackie Mason in 1979. The remainder of his career—hosting this open-mike night, appearing in used-car commercials, writing a humor column for a karaoke newsletter—made the Mason thing look like the happy fluke it was. After a week of informal tutoring, Louie pepped me up backstage (the bar kitchen, with the fry cook squeezing around us) on my first night. I was going on right after this other guy who called himself Fish McGill, a regular who did a lot of sight gags with his outsized tie. I should've taken it as an omen.

We sat on stools in the hot kitchen. Louie said, "You look nervous, friend. Don't be. There's no reason to be. If I've learned one thing in all my years of comedy, it's that nervousness is an empty concept." Louie was full of realizations and sage philosophies like this. His main one was this whole theory about mean laughter versus honest laughter. Go for the honest laughs, he always said. Those are the ones that count.

"That's incredibly reassuring."

"It's all in the head. Nobody's shooting nervous-beams at you, are they? *You* make yourself nervous. *You* control it. So what do *you* do?" He didn't give me a chance to answer. "*You* grab the dial and turn it down, friend."

It had already been turned down considerably, in fact, by three rum-and-Cokes. I took off my shirt.

"What is this about?"

"Part of the act," I said.

He smiled. "Follow your instincts if they lead you that way," he said, following me to the doorway. "And hey, no fag jokes."

So I went out on the tiny painted plywood stage and stood behind the mike, my white chest luminous in the light. "Man," I said, "I've been in Vegas for two weeks and, whoa, they weren't kidding when they said you can lose your shirt here."

Pitiful laughter. One pair of hands, clapping slowly like a taunt. I tugged my shirt on.

"Really, though. Gambling is a serious business. I read this article about how the casinos are starting to operate much like banks. In fact, many of them now have direct-deposit programs."

Nada. Think funeral. I cleared my throat against the dead air.

"But, really now, the competition is tough. They're upgrading all their attractions to draw bigger crowds. You know the Mirage volcano, how it erupts once an hour? Not enough in today's competitive casino market. Now they're going to sacrifice a virgin once an hour too."

Clinks of beer bottles, coughs, bathroom comings and goings.

Think cemetery in a vacuum. Louie bought the drinks afterward. Think consolation prize.

That first night, I left Bead's and caught a cab to the Strip. I was drunk and stubborn enough not to feel completely defeated yet, and so I wanted to walk under the lights of the casinos to see—in my naive belief that making a new start in a new city was a matter of conquest—what I was up against. The shadow of Dad was dogging me, too, demanding with a sneer that I prove myself.

And, of course, I wanted to gamble. I went into Treasure Island, gravitated toward a blackjack table and bought in with fifty bucks worth of chips. It was just me, the bald, skeletal dealer, and this old guy in a cowboy hat who looked like a grizzled ranch hand. Pretty soon I was up a hundred bucks and two more rum-and-Cokes. Instead of feeling good, though, I was feeling stupid and confessional.

"I'm a standup comedian," I said to the dealer. "More a disease than a profession at this point." He just blinked and smiled without showing his teeth. He continued flipping cards. The ranch hand just nodded; his snakeskin hatband glistened beneath the lights. "I just got here. Vegas, that is. Trying to break in, you know. To the business. Not your house." The dealer just smiled thinly, politely enforcing the silence. "Do you moonlight as a mime, or what?"

He smiled with teeth this time. "I'm sure you'll do fine here, sir," he said. It was a polite way of saying *can it, asshole.* A few hands and one blackjack later and I was up two hundred.

"Are you allowed to be yourself?" I asked the dealer. "You seem wound kind of tight."

"Card, sir?" His finger tapped the shiny deck.

"A smiling block of ice. Is that *really* you?" My head felt like a water balloon from the drinks. My dubious wit was souring. This always happened when I got toasty.

A low, phlegmy rumble came from my left. The ranch hand clearing his throat.

"If I tipped you a hundred bucks, then would you be yourself?"

The dealer said, "I'm as myself as I'm going to get, sir. Card, sir?"

The ranch hand grumbled, his voice all chewing tobacco and hay. "Trying to think over here."

"Sir?" The dealer looked at me with raised eyebrows.

I said I was sorry. "I just had my first night here doing standup. It didn't go too well."

The dealer said he was sorry to hear that, and then he slid more chips across the felt toward me. Two hundred twenty.

"Why do I keep winning?"

The dealer said I must be lucky in some things. Sir.

"But the important question," I said, clacking my chips, "is how an aspiring comedian breaks into the showrooms. You live here. You know how the machinery works. Deal me in. Heh-heh?"

Then the ranch hand said, "You want craps."

"Pardon me?"

All he needed was a piece of wheat in his mouth. "You keep talking. Craps is for talking people. Blackjack is for us quiet people."

"You're just mad because I keep winning."

Sir. The dealer.

"But, of course, you're gonna lose," I said to the ranch hand. "It's God's way of punishing you for humping your sister."

Ranch hand put his cards down and stood up. He was like a horse: when it gets up close, it's always bigger than you thought. He took the front of my shirt in his hand, as easy as if he was pulling up a handful of grass. "I'll gladly take you outside, mister." I was on my tiptoes, panting, with my lungs in my ears.

Sir. The dealer was talking to me.

A bubble of silence surrounded us. People stared. I took the hint. I cashed out with two hundred and fifty bucks. I stumbled outside and slowly sobered up into an upright walk. The lights became clear and small like earrings. Unlike the alcohol, the shame of failure at Bead's hadn't burned off. It clung like a sweaty shirt. I walked the Strip, mulled over my failure some more, walked some more, right into compromise. I concluded: six months. Make it here six months. Six months was enough to make my return home look like I'd *wanted* to come home, rather than *needed* to. Until then, three phone calls. Five postcards. A few hints. A week later I found a job delivering pizzas, got an apartment with walls thinner than my ego. I endured rap from next door thumping my spine until four A.M. most nights. I returned to Bead's open-mike night twice, just to make sure I had squeezed the last few drops of blood from my illusions. Oh, yes, indeed I had.

We finally took Officer Friendly's advice and went to the movies. Mom insisted on seeing this movie about Whoopi Goldberg working on this huge quilt for ten years to appease her husband's ghost, Dad wanted to catch an action thriller, and I'd have really rather hung in the lobby and paid quarters to shoot things. Of course, I had to work on Dad. When I followed him to the theater, he eyed me like I was trying to steal his wallet. He knew I wasn't into action thrillers. He had his guard up.

We fumbled around people and took our seats eight rows from the back.

I said, "Build any new contraptions lately?" My dad was always tinkering in the garage. He would fill vegetable cans with cement for paperweights, make model airplanes out of PVC pipe and beer cans. He would even fire up the lathe on occasion to machine motorcycle parts for retired friends. "I'm still waiting for your super-collider to come out. I want to direct your infomercial."

The previews were showing: vampires, improbably fiery car crashes, gunfights, frantic kisses, improbably large breasts.

He said, "Built a worm probe. Didn't really build it. Just an electrified nail on a stick. You know how it works?"

"Through electricity, I suppose." On the screen: More breasts. A tank. A giant time-traveling praying mantis.

"It slowly electrifies a contained area belowground, so the worms can't take it."

"So they wriggle out of the ground."

"Precisely."

"Cool. You should have lent that to the cops. They could've flushed out Red by now."

I thought I heard a faint chuckle. On the screen: A cartoon bear with nunchaku. A seven-year-old psychic girl. A train wreck. A reptile-woman with a bazooka.

He said, "How about you get some popcorn?"

I said sure, and waited a second. But he didn't move to get his wallet.

After the movie, we were on the road again. I was starting to wonder when I was ever going to get to plead my case. Doing it in front of Mom, I calculated, would be risky. She's a pushover, sure, and I could get her pity with one pouty downward turn of my mouth. Problem was that Dad knew I'd try to exploit such a strategy and he'd dig in his feet against me.

We stopped at a Tacos Guapos downtown. We sat in a booth and poked and nibbled at our steaming outsized burritos while mariachi music blared from a pink jukebox.

"I think we should go back after this," Mom said. "Three hours is plenty of time. It's funny how it takes much longer than you'd think. After you watch *Cops*, you think everything for them is a new little episode that they can wrap up in a few minutes."

Dad shook his head. "You don't have the slightest idea how that show works."

"Of course I do. Cameraman goes out with police, cameraman films what happens. It's simple. That's why people like it so much."

"It's not that simple," he said. "You don't understand how edited that show is. It only seems like they take a few minutes. It's never that way in real life. You don't understand that real life is much messier than that."

"I know that, Joe. That's exactly what I was saying."

"You didn't make yourself very clear."

"Jason understood what I was saying."

"Transmission received. I want to inform you my burrito growls every time I fork it."

"What does he know?" Dad said. "Your son thinks he's going to make a living as a standup comedian."

"Actually, I was getting tired standing on stage. So now I'm the world's first sit-down comedian."

Dad shook his head. "Christ."

Mom patted my arm.

"Of course, I'm about ready for another career change." We could be out driving all night. Dad was grumpy, but I was supposed to leave in the morning. I had to do something.

"You mastered comedy, did you? Too clever for me, I guess," he said.

"Joe."

"For my next career move, I'm thinking of becoming a Greek philosopher. I got fitted for robes and sandals last week."

"You always were a thoughtful person," Mom said. "You used to read so much. Don't forget your hemlock and library card."

I said, "I'm still missing a few things. A benefactor."

Dad looked up.

"What do you mean?" Mom said.

Dad chewed, watching me. He knew.

"Well, I certainly can't afford all these olive crowns and hemlock on my own. And I need to cultivate a circle of young admirers. Preferably nubile teens. I need investors. Support. What do you think of that? A philosophy major backed by the Dad Corp." In my head, I was promising to finish school, full credit load, straight A's, please, Dad, please.

He looked at me with his deep-set brown eyes. A smile flickered on his greasy lips. He said slowly, "That is the funniest thing you said all night."

"Did I miss a joke?" Mom said.

"The one about the philosopher needing investors. Ha." His smile was genuine. He enjoyed this. Meanwhile, my heart was traveling toward my left ankle.

Mom said, "Joe, you need a nap." She was going to say something else—plead my case?—but then she didn't say anything.

We finished eating in cramped silence. I just wanted to go home. We filed back to the truck. Before he opened his door, Dad said to me, by way of gloating epilogue, "It's all just like some comic strip to you, son. Some big cartoon. I've got news for you."

"Don't even say it."

"Good," he said. "Then we're finished with it."

I knew as we neared the neighborhood that the standoff still wasn't over, because now people were sitting in lawn chairs in their front yards and drinking beer, a few radios blaring senselessly. Firecrackers spattered and people laughed. Everybody was turning the spectacle into a party. I bet half of them didn't even know what was happening.

We cruised toward our street and, just as I'd expected, that yellow tape still stretched across Edith Avenue, telling us DO NOT CROSS. But Dad said he didn't mind; he said he wouldn't mind driving around and hearing some more of my material. Funny stuff like that philosopher joke. Ha ha. Maybe I *did* have a shot in the comedy business, he said.

I thought, Fuck you and your mean little laughter. I hope you have to drive around all night. It would have been funny if the standoff had actually ended hours ago and the police had just forgotten to take the yellow tape down. Red would be working on his Mustang in the garage with his friends, in an empty neighborhood where he could live on his own terms. One time I heard his friends razz him for working on his Mustang all the time. "If it ain't broke, tune it up," he said. "Tweak that motherfucker till it purrs."

But who knew what was happening. Maybe his wife was pleading with the cops on his behalf now. Red made mistakes, but Judy always forgave him. And, judging from the frequency of the Jacuzzi ritual, she had to be forgiving on a regular schedule. Hell, I found myself forgiving Red, even if he had threatened Judy's life, even if he had driven us out of our home for the night, even if it wasn't until three in the morning that we got back (strangely, police tape still webbed around his yard) and I stuffed back into my duffel bag the shirts I'd been stupid enough to secretly hang up in the closet of my old room. And, despite what Mom said about this whole episode being good material, if I ever went back to comedy, I would never make jokes about Red, that was for sure. There wasn't anything funny about his situation: the next morning as I stood in the kitchen with my duffel bag, about to say good-bye for who knew how long, my mother handed me a folded section of the morning paper. The article said Judy and Debbie had got out of the house okay, but Red refused to surrender. The cops finally teargassed his house. They shot and killed him when he came out firing.

Then she saw I had my duffel bag. "You going home right this instant?"

"I think so," I said.

Sometimes I amaze even myself with the shit I wisecrack about. But when I saw that article about Red, I just stood there, blank, emptied out. No jokes here. And what Louie had told me suddenly clicked. Comedians shouldn't dispense with compassion. You shouldn't be unfeeling or crude. The laughs you got from taking that route were small and shallow. They were mean little laughs, not honest laughs. Targeting people with troubles—wronged working men, the dead, young exiles stuck between home and nowhere—was no way to make people laugh, I mean really, truly laugh. Those mean little laughs weren't a form of joy, but a kind of smiling hostility that said, I am better than you. I win. You lose. Now get out of my face and don't come back. Ha ha ha.

The Fish Magician

DAVID KRANES

1

Malcolm hears the call, the invitation, and rises from his seat, his wife's, Ginger's, hand like a heat phantom floating in the air behind him—pushing him forward? staying him? It's hard to tell. And now Malcolm climbs stairs, mounts the stage, says *hello* to the thin magician, shakes hands, steps into a box windowed by Lucite, pinned by light. And—seeing the man with the cape furl something huge and purple, something velveteen, up and into the air over the box (if there is sound—sound hushed), then seeing no more, seeing nothing because seeing leaps beyond vision, becomes gemcolor before it's anything seen, some essential ardor of emerald, ruby, some hardcolor truth in a gale wind that sucks every bone into his breath, Malcolm feels himself hurled, then hurled—somewhere north, north off of the stage, out of the theater, casino, resort: out of town, finally, across one state line, possibly two, where it smells like juniper, a thousand edgeless rocks, heron feathers. One can imagine Idaho. Why not? A sign, print burned into wood, then stained, says, MAGIC RESERVOIR. Why not. Malcolm listens for clues and hears only a world-beyond-traffic.

2

All I ever wanted to be was funny. But fate deals. They call sports the gateway into whatever you'd do if you had brains or talent. So I was a second-string all-American, playing four years with the Cincinnati Bengals, four more with the San Diego Chargers. Truth's funny when you say it right. And we get second chances. So funny was what I tried to be broadcasting *Monday Night Football*

with The Fatman and The Prince of Nose Candy, but the network
saw what-I-thought-hilarious differently, told me *shut up or leave*.
Be reasonable—right? How does a broadcaster shut up? So I left,
made a little noise, went on talk shows for a year—did you know
Boomer Esiason?—never mind—got sued twice, run down by a car
(not an accident), body knocked into a ditch in a remote Saskatche-
wan I-think-the-word-is-*village*. For a week I was the missing body.
But then I regained what I've realized, since then, is *more*-than-
consciousness, found myself, climbed up onto the road, *got* found,
came here, and, now, do what I do: try to *employ* my more-than-
consciousness, find other people, audition, do the comedy clubs.

True story: I'm taking lunch at the Mirage California Pizza
Kitchen so I can watch the sports book with a pair of hundred-
power Bushnells, and this woman comes up—handsome, mid-
forties, jewelry, nicely accessorized—asks am I who I am? is my
casebook full? Good because she has a missing body.

The missing body's her husband. They went to see Lance Burton
at the Monte Carlo last night. Great show! she said; great show!
have you seen it? Of course. Somewhere around—she had looked at
her watch—10:45, Lance asks for someone in the audience. Woman's husband's a magic freak, been one since he was a kid, pops up
out of his showroom seat, goes up, steps into a box; Lance makes
him disappear, does seven other tricks, levitates himself on a motorcycle, road-trips the air—blue smoke. The show ends, theater emp-
ties. My lady's waiting; waiting. She's the only one in the theater
except a stagehand; he says, *Ma'am?* She says, *Lance Burton made
my husband—my husband, Malcolm—disappear; where would he—?*
Stagehand has no idea. *Wait here,* he says. It's five, ten, fifteen
minutes. Man comes out in a suit, looks very casino: *Would you
come with me?* he asks. My lady follows; the two go to an office.
Clearly executive, clearly management; office is like a suite, full bar,
entertainment center; *What would you like to drink?* the executive
asks. *Any pirozhki? dolmas?* She repeats her story: *Where's my husband? Sit down,* the executive suit asks. *Please. I need to explain
something,* but first he makes her sign saying all he tells her will be
held in strictest confidence.

She does. She tells me: as much of a suit as the executive is, the
guy is shaking; he's a man probably plays golf six out of seven and

he's white. *Something tragic is happening,* he says. Lance Burton—
one of the great magicians of the world and for whom the Monte
Carlo built and designed their present showroom—has incipient
Alzheimer's. *Hands are fine,* executive says; *skill . . . skill's as nimble
as ever. The man* defines *"dexterous." Short term, though, is another
matter. Where's my husband?* my lady asks. *We wish we knew,* the
executive says. *I asked Lance: "Lance: you remember making the
gentleman in the black turtleneck, brown houndstooth disappear?"
He said, "Yes." I asked, "So, do you remember where you disappeared
him to?" Trust me: Lance feels terrible. He feels humiliated. He
knows this is happening to him. And I have to tell you: it's unforgiv-
ing; it's cruel. One of the great magicians of the world.*

You learn to ask the obvious: Where does Lance disappear most of
his things, people? What my lady'd been told was, *Different places.*
Like—? Apparently, there's no pattern. That was part of Lance's fun.
Sometimes the balcony of the showroom. Sometimes backstage.
Sometimes across the street to the MGM. The further away, the
more the challenge is what Lance had said. And in the last year—
almost to defy his loss of memory—he'd pushed. One time he'd
made a horse disappear, and the horse showed up on the stage with
Rosie O'Donnell in Atlantic City. Could I help? My lady had asked
around, and I had a certain infamy for missing bodies. She'd read
the hack piece in *Sports Illustrated* about the network firing me and
how that had led, in ways, to my finding missing bodies. The Monte
Carlo would pay. Would I talk to Lance? Would I take the case?

One of the funniest books in the Old Testament, I think, is Job.
His boils kill me. It cracks me up how Job says, "Let the night be
solitary." How do you come up with a line like that? Job's like Chap-
lin; he's like this ancient Little Tramp who can't get anything; it's
a riot. Chapter 10 is like comic genius. Verse 10: "Hast thou not
poured me out as milk, curdled me like cheese?" I mean, it's just one
of those things that is funny—in the way Wisconsin is funny. Except
I would have ended Job differently. In chapter 41 and cut chapter
42, had it end where the darts are counted as stubble and he's
laughing at a shaking spear. I'm working up a whole Job routine,
and I wouldn't mind being warm-up at the Monte Carlo.

So I say, Yes: *Have the Monte Carlo call Lance.* Also, have them
agree: the missing body in return for one night in Lance's Evening

of Magic. *Do you have even an intuition?* my lady asks. I see fields of mission-bell, bitterroot. *Idaho,* I say. *Idaho?* she puzzles. *But there's no connection; we have no connection whatsoever with Idaho; we've never been. All the more reason for the intuition,* I say.

Lance is at a loss when, over the phone, I take him through guided imagery.

His voice sags on all the unaccented syllables. He tries, *but . . .* Which is so many people—isn't it? Still, he comes up with post-cards: lava rock, watercress, a blue heron. *I'm missing a dove,* he tells me, *a small water fountain . . . half an assistant. I'll keep my eyes out,* I tell him. A dove, a small fountain, half an assistant—lava rock, watercress, a blue heron. I take the elevator to the top of the Strato-sphere, walk around and around the observation deck. I call my lady, whose name is Ginger. *Any word?* I ask. *The phone rings—then Whoever hangs up,* she says; *any chance it's Malcolm?* It's the Monte Carlo, seeing if she's still in town, but I don't say that.

I take a cab up the Boulevard, walk around backstage, get let into the Magic Room, touch boxes, blades of swords, birdcages. *Idaho!* everything whispers—like sex, like the relics of saints—*Idaho!* There are three blood-carpeted stairs to a small platform; I climb them. I disappear, just for a moment, then reappear again. My breathing's shallow, rock-washed, filled with ozone. I leave the Magic Room, call Ginger. *Meet me at Sfuzzi,* I say, *seven o'clock, in the Fashion Show Mall. It's across from The Dive.*

I root out Ginger's executive-in-charge—a man with sunken eyes, sunken cheeks, and a nose that's listing. I say, *Mr. Castelli: I need an hour with Lance.* Castelli's voice wants to scramble my signal. He's all distrust-pretending-to-be-cooperation. He says, *I guess; okay; if a lawyer's present. But don't get any ideas; you're going to have to* prove *magical negligence.*

Lance Burton's by his pool, *with* lawyer. The air's sheeted like phyllo; light's like lava rock. *Make something disappear,* I ask. I'm just trying to find a handle. *It doesn't have to be difficult; anything.* He chooses the water in the pool; it's gone; the pool's dry; then it's back again. *Interesting,* I say. *Do it again. Something else.* He's wearing a bathing suit with fish. The fish disappear; it's a solid blue suit; then the rainbows are back again. *One more time,* I request. He's eating a salad. He waves his hand, and that's the end of the watercress; it's just radicchio. *You're good,* I say; *that's the word on the street and I can't dispute it. Bring the watercress back.* Lance Burton says, *Bring the* what *back?* and the lawyer whispers something into his ear.

We do word association and it might as well be sandblasting. I say *coriander;* he says *sigmoidoscopy.* I ask: had he ever seen Malcolm prior to last night—in a videotape, perhaps, photograph? Any prior conversations with Malcolm's Ginger? The Monte Carlo lawyer leans in, whispers. *We take exception to your implications,* he says. *Mr. Burton's no* hit *magician.* I say, *Except he* is *a hit magician,* and though it's reasonably quick, it's not funny.

I meet Ginger at Sfuzzi. When the hostess asks: *inside or outside,* I say: *it's the story of my life.* Ginger prefers *inside*—where she feels *more volume,* she says, *more shape.* They have conditioner ducts the color of jicama. We split an *insalata mista* and I order a bottle of Marilyn Merlot—you take your laughs wherever. *What've you found out?* Ginger asks, and in this particular night—full moon, Strip traffic like gelatin, the sound of The Dive next door hitting the bottom of the ocean—*What've-you-found-out?* seems such a delicious question.

I have a theory about Inevitability. Greek tragedy used to be comedy before it was tragedy. The House of Atreus was originally a fun house; something happened to the mirrors; Sophocles broke one of the mirrors, then figured *fuckit,* broke them all. Discoveries used to be marriages before they were blindings; people spilled wine, not blood; professional football used to be professional magic before special teams. It's the mirror thing all over—again and again. Back at the beginning, fish had feathers.

So: *what had I found out?* Ginger had Merlot on her upper lip, the unwashed crust of a crying jag on one cheekbone. Bodies get lost— isn't that amazing?!—but not forever. That you can find the missing body again and again is, I think, a miracle. *What had I found out?*

—It's indisputable, I say.

—What's indisputable?

—Idaho.

—Idaho's indisputable?

—Absolutely.

—How can Idaho be indisputable?

I say—you're wild, Ginger.
She says—seriously.
I say—because: look at us; look at where we are.
She says—yes.
I say—smell the night.
She does.
I say—Idaho's the next state.

3

Malcolm supports himself against a lodgepole at the foot of the spillway. *I was somewhere,* he thinks; *somewhere in a world not here—where* was *that?* Folded on the stones are his black turtleneck, brown houndstooth. There are plovers, stellar jays on branches. Indigo buntings browse the ground thatch: *seeds?* with each inquiry of beak: *seeds? seeds?* The water falling sounds like applause.

Where was it that he . . . ? Memory, in this place, seems very much like a binnacle in a kitchen in Oklahoma—a thing unnecessary. Malcolm thinks: *the inevitability of water! comedy of light!* and he forgoes connection—because there are open birdcages in a logjam of tamarack and black hawthorn, nesting cinnamon teal; rock dove. And there's a small fountain lodged in a listing Engleman. Colored scarves blow by like sheeting rain. And in a field beyond which horses dance, field rife with Russian thistle, is half a woman. Upper.

—Oh, my dear! Malcolm says.

—Hello! the half-woman says. —Take a card-any-card! My name's Sheila!

—What happened? Malcolm says.

—Isn't this all wonderful? Sheila says. —Finally? At last?!

—But you're only half-here, Malcolm says.

—For *me:* at *least* I'm half-here, Sheila says. And then—Look! oh, look! and points, and a purple cape floats by on the Big Wood River.

Then two others—man, woman—climb the horizon of barbed wire, up over what-seems-a-stairway down: the man, a man over-burdened with sinew and lank; the woman's wrists mirrors of atmosphere. Between them—a picnic basket and boom box. The boom box plays Kenny G.

—Ginger! Malcolm says.

—Idaho! Ginger says.

And the lank man, wishing-he-could-be-funny-only, points behind, to a point where the two climbed. —*Sportsman's Access,* he says. —It says *Magic Reservoir/Sportsman's Access.*

The Night Uncle Willy's Car Caught on Fire on the I-95

RICHARD LOGSDON

1

Right in the middle of hell—that's where Uncle Willy Parker thought he was. It was 11:30 P.M. in late November. Willy squatted in the emergency parking lane of the I-95 freeway that snaked through Las Vegas. He was about five hundred feet from his car, which was being eaten by an angry ball of flame.

Jesus, thought Willy, things can't get much worse than this.

He inhaled deeply on his cigarette and looked at a small white surveyor's circle on the asphalt below him. My life's like that spot, Willy thought: a big damned zero. A man with a receding hairline who tied his dirty brown hair in a ponytail, Willy knew he had seen better days, but he couldn't remember many. Tonight, he wore a leather jacket, a black T-shirt with a red OZZIE RULES on the chest, and Levi's. He could almost feel the heat coming through the pavement under his feet and thought of removing his black boots.

To Willy, watching the flames consume a car that had served as a second home (particularly when he took off to gamble in Pahrump, just outside of Vegas) was like seeing God's judgment firsthand. Shivering, he remembered sitting with his mother years ago in the old Bruce Street church and listening to blind Preacher Ray's sermons on the wrath of the Almighty. A tall black man with graying hair, Ray had frequently described the Good Lord as an all-consuming fire. Willy could remember Ray standing in front of the congregation—made of drifters, dealers, prostitutes, teachers, and lawyers—holding up his floppy brown leather Bible and proclaiming the Word. During the sermons, young Willy had hung on Ray's every word.

Thinking of how he missed Ray, Willy sucked on his last Lucky Strike. He felt like a man facing a firing squad, and he figured he was under a curse. Things had gone to hell in the past five years with his ex-wife Rachel dying from a stroke and his having to spend time in the state pen for attempted robbery.

Thirty minutes ago Willy had left the downtown parking lot of Crazy Luck Casino, where he had gotten drunk and gambled away most of his paycheck at the blackjack tables. Bringing his car up to fifty, he had just entered the freeway headed southeast toward Amber's apartment when he had smelled smoke and seen flames shooting through the floorboard and from under the hood of his primer-gray '76 Chevrolet. Almost as if he were prepared for catastrophe, Willy had calmly pulled over to the side of the freeway and, leaving the car running in neutral, had gotten out and walked away. Willy didn't much care if the car, a gift from his daddy, exploded with him ten feet away. He had steadily maintained the car since his daddy's death.

Squatting in the November night, Willy watched his car explode, throwing metal and glass fragments into the air. Sighing, he recalled his daddy's death and wondered, anguished, if there was some sort of cosmic connection here.

2

The exploding car brought back the memory of the day Fred Parker had departed this planet. A vicious son of a bitch in the opinion of all who knew him, his daddy had been Willy's best and only friend. Just before Fred's apocalyptic exit on New Year's Day, Willy had been sprawled on the faded green couch in the living room of his father's house, his two overweight and redheaded boys, Runt and Spike, lying on the floor in front of him. Having had her fill of New Year's at the Parker house, Willy's beautiful redheaded wife, Rachel, had decided to spend the day with her parents.

Willy and his boys had been watching the bowl games when his daddy had disappeared. A balding, gap-toothed, marijuana-smoking old man who, stooped by age, still towered over everyone else in the family, his daddy had put on his black boots and shuffled out to the kitchen to get himself and Willy a couple of cold ones from the old white Westinghouse Frigidaire. In the Parker family, even when his momma was still alive (she had died in a head-on automobile accident the day Willy became the first Parker to graduate high school) and all the Parkers and Remingtons had gathered in the old house on D Street to celebrate, New Year's Day had always meant drinking as much beer as you could between twelve and twelve.

When the oven exploded with a loud *ka-whoom!*, taking Daddy with it in a fury of gas and flame, Uncle Willy had at first imagined that the sound had come from the TV set. After all, it was halftime at the Orange Bowl, and to please his sons—both had their earphones on so they could listen to tapes while watching TV—Willy had turned the set way up so that he could barely hear himself think. And, after drinking twelve brewskies, Uncle Willy hadn't given his daddy's absence much thought until the end of the third period, when it looked like Alabama might win by at least thirty.

Finally, thirsty and impatient, smelling smoke from wood but thinking nothing of it, Willy had pushed himself off the sofa and headed to the kitchen, calling out, "Daddy, Daddy, where's my damned beer at?" When he slowly stepped through the splintered wooden door that had once separated his mother's kitchen kingdom from everything else in the house, he nearly vomited at the amount of blood on the walls, ceiling, and counter and from the gas and smoke fumes that had not yet spilled out of the three shattered windows.

Feeling that a significant period of his life had just gone up in smoke, Willy stood still and tried to take it all in. One look at the oven, blackened from flame, told Willy what had likely occurred: opening the door of the gas oven to take a peek at the turkey, Daddy had lit another doobie, forgetting that while he had turned on the gas more than an hour ago he had neglected to put in the bird, which even now remained in the refrigerator.

Wishing he hadn't drunk so much, Uncle Willy squatted on the tiled floor, studying the scene, as his two sons walked in. All that remained of Fred Parker were his two black cowboy boots, now smoldering in the middle of the floor. "Jesus Christ!" Willy exclaimed, a tear in his eye, feeling slightly religious and wondering if he should pray or call the cops. "Jesus H. Christ. I guess that's the end o' Daddy." Willy reached into his shirt pocket, pulled out a Lucky Strike, and lit it up. He inhaled and tried to collect his thoughts.

Still wearing their headphones, Runt and Spike stood next to their father, surveying the scene unmoved, as if they had seen similar disasters a thousand times before.

"Grandpa was sure a mean fucker, huh? Guess I'm gonna miss the ol' bastard," the eleven-year-old Spike yodeled, wiping his nose with the back of his hand and staring at the smoking boots.

"Oh, well, ya gotta go sooner or later is what I always say. Speakin' of which: I guess it's time for us to go home, huh, Paps?" was all Runt, the older one, said. Instinctively, Willy stood and smacked the obese thirteen-year-old on the side of the head with his open hand, sending the boy's headphones clattering to the floor. It's what Fred would have done to Willy when Willy was a boy.

"Yeow!!" Runt screamed like a mountain cat and rubbed the side of his head before bending over to pick up his phones. "What was that for, Daddy?"

Willy scratched his head, looked down at his sons, glanced at the boots, and wondered what to do.

Then, after striding across the kitchen, opening the refrigerator, and grabbing the turkey, Willy pushed both boys out of the kitchen, out of the front door of the house, and drove back to their trailer home in North Las Vegas. When Willy got home and sobered up a bit, he called Preacher and asked him what to do. Following Preacher Ray's advice, which was always sound, if not scriptural, Willy finally phoned the emergency number and tried to stay up waiting for Rachel to come home and put the kids to bed. But she never came. By the next night, when Rachel returned home and said she had found another man, the incident had made the evening news. Three days later, Rachel packed her bags, left Willy and his sons, and moved in with her boyfriend in Pahrump.

3

Willy's thoughts hurtled like a meteor back to the present, where he squatted in the cold, windy November night and watched his car burn.

"I coulda been in that fuckin' car," Willy mumbled and stood, searching his pants and coat pockets for another pack of Lucky Strikes, a flask of whiskey, anything to steady his nerves. All he found was the small loaded pistol that he carried for protection.

"And if I hadda been in that car," Willy added, aware that no one but the Lord Above was listening, "I woulda been dancin' with Daddy and the angels right now." The thought of being reunited with Fred Parker made Willy sad and glad. Even though he loved Amber, his thirty-five-year-old girlfriend, who made enough money dancing nude at the bar for both of them, Willy still missed his daddy.

Catlike now, Willy crouched in the darkness, the full moon overhead, and wondered what to do. The fire had begun to die out, leaving the gray and charred frame of his car resembling a skeleton. He wondered how he could live his life from this point on.

Suddenly, Willy had a personal revelation. Looking over the years, he saw his life as a blackboard design, bracketed by two fiery incidents, with a lot of small fires in between. In '88, five years after Fred Parker had given up the ghost, Runt had been gunned down at a 7-Eleven over on Rancho. Then, running guns somewhere in Central America, Spike had contracted malaria and died on New Year's Day of '93. Ninety-three was the year Willy's ex had died, too. Willy's life seemed caught in a holding pattern.

In '95, Willy had found Amber, or rather Amber had found him.

Seeing him sitting alone in the corner of a seedy North Las Vegas bar, she had approached the loner with the ponytail, asked him if he wanted her to dance for him, and toward the end of the evening had asked Willy to drive her home. Willy figured that Amber was desperate for a man; in reality, Amber, a curvaceous blond with blood-red lips and an empty head, had felt sorry for Willy because none of the other girls in the club would touch him. His parents, children, and car now gone, Amber was all he had left on this earth.

He wondered what Preacher Ray was doing now. Since it was Saturday night, he knew that the pastor—if he was still alive—would be preparing for a day of worship. Ray had said some of the best things Willy had ever heard. For a blind man, Preacher's insistence that people take care of each other had made a lot of sense. "You are your brother's and your sister's and your mother's and your father's keeper!" Ray had often proclaimed, randomly pointing at a member of the congregation. When Willy had left the church years ago, Ray had kept in touch and had affectionately referred to him as "the sheep that wandered." Willy wondered what Ray, that old floppy Bible in his hand, would tell him to do now. For a second, Willy thought of using what change he had left to call the old man for guidance.

But just as suddenly, he changed his mind, particularly when he saw the police cruiser, its reds and blues flashing, pull up behind the smoldering remains of his car. Willy hated cops. As the two patrolmen got out of the squad car, walked over to and then around what remained of his Chevrolet, Willy realized that he hadn't been seen. He knew that if he did approach the cops, they would take his name, ask for ID, and do a computer check. Then they'd know about Willy's long-standing warrant, and that would mean at least a year in the slammer.

No, sir, I sure as hell do not want that, Willy thought, feeling the small bulge of his pistol in his jacket pocket. I sure as hell do not want that. Promising to himself to call Amber tomorrow, Willy walked to the concrete barrier on the side of the freeway and put one leg over it. Chilled by the wind, he looked back at the cops, who appeared to be searching for an ID number on the body of the car, and then looked below at the darkened apartment complexes, houses, and stores of one of the oldest, most crime-infested neighborhoods in the Southwest. A week ago, the body of an old high school acquaintance, Billy Smith, had been found in a Dumpster out behind a Mexican restaurant Willy used to take his kids to. Willy figured he had no choice, and, putting the other leg over the concrete barrier, he walked and slid down the rocky dirt embankment to the vacant lot below. As he reached the bottom, dust billowing around him and covering his clothes in a gritty film, he could see some human shapes shuffling through the lot. Looking across the lot, he noticed two or three people milling in front of Leroy's 24-hour liquor store.

Reassuring himself that his gun was loaded, Willy started off across the lot. Walking against the cold wind, he knew that things could only get better.

4

As Willy entered the liquor store through its large glass door, his hand on his pistol, the tall, stooped, gray-haired black man standing behind the counter gave him a malicious look. This must be Leroy, Willy thought, and Leroy's got fire in his eyes. For an instant, the old man reminded Willy of his daddy: same height, same squinting mean brown eyes, same thin and gangly build. Hesitating for a moment, keeping his hand on the gun, Willy tried to look mean right back, then knew that he could not shoot this man. His life a chain of big and small fires, Willy felt tired, defeated, and wanted to rest. He wanted to put the fires out once and for all.

"The fuck you want here?" the old man bellowed, not batting an eye, undaunted by Willy's presence. Stunned, Willy said nothing.

"What you want I asked you!!!" This time, the man screamed at Willy. His hands under the counter separating himself from the rest of the store, the grizzled old man glanced at Willy's right arm, saw Willy's hand stuffed into the side pocket of his jacket. "You got a gun in there, you piece of shit? You got a gun, you white son of a bitch? 'Cause you do, you do, motherfucker, you shoulda used it soon as you come steppin' through that door."

Willy froze as he saw the old man slowly bring his hands above the counter, saw Leroy cushion the stock of the gun against his shoulder, saw the sawed-off shotgun aimed at his chest, yelled something, felt the force of the shotgun's blast even before he heard the gun's deafening explosion, wondered if he was in a dream as he flew backwards into and through the glass door, shattering the thick glass like it was thin ice, feeling himself land like a feather on the concrete of the store's entrance.

Lying on the pavement, his head on concrete and glass, Uncle Willy felt no pain, only a light chilling sensation moving through his body, and he knew he was struggling to breathe. He was suffocating. This has to be a dream, he thought to himself; this has gotta be a damned dream. Willy didn't feel anything as he somehow commanded his left hand to move to his chest and then to a spot in front of his face. His hand covered with blood, Willy realized that he had been shot and was probably dying.

Uncle Willy Parker tried to catch his breath again and again, but no matter how hard he tried, he was suffocating. Unable to raise his head, Willy looked at the full moon straight above him, then saw the old black man's face in place of the moon. This must be Leroy, my executioner, Willy thought, struggling for breath.

Closing his eyes while fighting for a final breath, Willy thought of his car burning on the freeway, of Amber dancing nude at the club, of his boys' laughter, and he now wished he had called Preacher Ray. The Preacher would have known what to do. Too, Willy realized that his hour of judgment had arrived.

This is it, Willy thought.

As he sensed light fade and darkness descend like an iron cloak, Willy opened his eyes one last time and could just make out the face of Fred Parker in the place where the moon had been. Willy had waited for this moment a long time, and he smiled.

"Hello, Daddy," Willy rasped, breathing his last and wondering what had taken his father so long to get back to him.

Insufficient Funds

MATTHEW O'BRIEN

In the reflection of his computer monitor, Nick Costello could see himself clearly. His shoulders sloped from a white tank top, and his stubby neck merged with a parabola-shaped chin. A goatee shaded his lips, which, if visible, would've been neither pouting nor smiling. His eyes were as dull and flat as cardboard, and a stretching pale streak—his forehead—hinted that his hairline was retreating. If his appearance called to mind any familiar image, it was that of someone who'd received bad news and not yet come to terms with it.

Nick flipped on the computer, and his reflection disappeared. As he reached for a cup of coffee teetering on the edge of the desk, his wife, Pam, emerged from the bathroom, wrapped in a towel. She hurried to the closet and began dressing.

"What time is it, Nicky?" she asked.

Nick glanced at the monitor. "Eight forty," he answered in a New York accent.

"Goddammit," she exclaimed, throwing her towel to the floor and rushing back into the bathroom. Nick could hear her rifling through her cosmetic case.

"Ya taking the boys with ya?" he asked.

After a long pause, she responded, "Yeah. I'm gonna drop them off at Grandma's, then go back over there after work. She wants us all to eat together tonight. Can you meet us over there?"

"Yeah," said Nick, unenthusiastically. "I got work to do, but I should be done by seven or so."

Pam reentered the bedroom and rushed to a dresser. She removed an apron and waiter's pad from the bottom drawer, then stuffed them in her purse. While putting on a pair of earrings, she turned to Nick.

"Did you pay the power bill, honey?"

"Not yet," he answered, staring at the screen. "I'll take care of it Monday."

"It was due two days ago, Nicky."

"Don't worry about it. I said I'll take care of it."

Pam dabbed her lips with a tissue, then gathered her purse. After ducking into the bathroom again, she left the room without speaking.

When Nick heard Pam and their two children exit the apartment, he double-clicked on the Sportsmaster icon. Betting lines started scrolling across the screen: Miami -1 NEW JERSEY, WASHINGTON -12 Dallas, CHARLOTTE -12 Orlando, CHICAGO -15 Sacramento. . . . The college lines soon followed: MARQUETTE -6 Memphis, VILLANOVA -2 Rutgers, ARIZONA -10 Stanford, Kentucky -2 SOUTH CAROLINA. . . .

Nick eyed the lines casually, then lunged for a black folder. While flipping through its pages, he guided the mouse to a pull-down menu, highlighted "Las Vegas Hilton," and clicked. Immediately more lines began moving across the screen: PROVIDENCE -5 Notre Dame, MISSISSIPPI -16 Auburn, Baylor -2 TEXAS A&M, FLORIDA ST. -10 Virginia. . . .

Nick observed the Hilton line for a full rotation, then frisked the desktop. Under a faded sports page, he found two pens—one red, one black—and began charting the numbers on a grid in the folder. Any variation from the overnight line he marked in red, all other numbers black. He wrote quickly and with purpose, eyes shifting from the screen to the folder, then back to the screen. After completing the top row of the grid—forty-three games total—he began charting the Stardust opening line in the same manner.

Once he had charted all the lines that had been released, Nick jumped in the shower. While drying off, he returned to his desk to see if any additional numbers had been posted. Bally's and MGM Grand had released their lines, but Imperial Palace, the Mirage, and Doc's, the Caribbean book he had an account with, had not. Nick could do without the numbers from Imperial Palace and the Mirage, but he had to have the line from Doc's. Its fluctuations told him what was happening on the East Coast, and he needed to know where the New York, Philly, Boston, and D.C. money was going. He glanced anxiously at the clock, then took his time getting dressed.

When Nick returned to his desk, all the opening lines had been released. Relieved, he charted them quickly, then slammed the folder shut. He then collected his wallet and keys and exited the apartment.

During hot streaks, Nick ate breakfast at a nearby Carrows Restaurant, where his wife worked as a waitress. When things weren't going so well, he dined elsewhere. On this particular day, he chose Denny's. Once settled in a corner booth, he peeled the sports section from a newspaper and opened it on the table. He perused the game stories and transactions, then studied the NBA box scores. The previous night he'd gone one for three and lost $600. He looked at the Indiana Pacers' box. He'd laid $550 on the Pacers, -6 at home against Charlotte; they only won by four. He eyed the minutes played column, then field goals made, field goals attempted, and free throws. He paused at the free throws column. As a team, the Pacers had converted only thirteen of twenty-three. He did the math in his head; he'd become quite good with numbers. If they would've shot 70 percent from the line—the NBA average—I would've covered the game, he determined angrily. That's a $1,050 swing. Instead of winning $450 for the night, I lost $600.

The waitress set Nick's food on the table, topped off his coffee, then walked away. He leaned the sports page against a bottle of ketchup and glanced at a section labeled "Today's Games." Miami at New Jersey. Dallas at Washington. Orlando at Charlotte. Sacramento at Chicago. He briefly analyzed the Kings/Bulls game: Sacramento had last night off, while Chicago narrowly defeated the Hawks in Atlanta. The Kings are on a three-game losing streak; the Bulls have won four in a row. Injuries? Each team is missing a starter and two key reserves. Last night, after all the results were in, Nick handicapped the game at -13. He was tempted to take the 15 but unwilling to go against the Bulls. Tonight he needed a sure thing, a lock. Tonight the pressure was on him, not the players. These guys don't know what pressure is, he thought, sipping his coffee. Pressure is having twenty bills to pay a month; pressure is when the rent's due in two days and you don't have half of it; collectors banging on your door is pressure.

He set his cup gently on the table. You don't get rich betting against the Bulls, he reasoned. Stay the hell away from that game; there are plenty of others on the board. For every twenty games posted, there's always one sure play. He remembered Vic Cherrone, an older guy he was once in a betting group with, telling him that. Today there were forty-three games available, so Nick guessed there were two solid plays, possibly three. But you only need to find one of them, he reminded himself. "Only one," he whispered, reaching for the check.

Once back at his apartment, Nick scribbled some notes in the folder, then charted the latest lines. There was very little movement. Chicago had dropped a point at the Las Vegas Hilton and the Mirage, and Villanova, which was hosting Rutgers, had jumped to -4 at Imperial Palace and the Stardust. A handful of other games had shifted a half point, but nothing dramatic, nothing peculiar.

With the folder opened on his lap, Nick guided the mouse to a pull-down menu, highlighted "NBA Matchups," and clicked. All of the day's games appeared on the screen in capsule form, complete with stats, streaks, trends, and injuries. Miami had covered four of the last five in New Jersey against the spread. Nick wrote this in the folder. San Antonio had won six in a row against Philadelphia. This was also noted. Chicago had shot 56 percent from the floor over its last ten games. . . .

Nick next perused the college capsules. Kentucky point guard Wayne Turner was questionable for tonight's game at South Carolina. Nick noted this at the bottom of the grid in red ink. Indiana's covered ten of the last thirteen games as a road dog. Disregard, Nick decided. This was a different Hoosier club from years past. Michigan was 35–5 in the last forty games in Ann Arbor. . . .

Nick spent more than two hours at his computer. He went online and visited several team and conference Web sites, scouring for injuries and suspensions. He also made a couple of phone calls, one to an assistant coach he'd befriended, the other to a fellow handicapper. Having narrowed his focus to twelve games, he placed the folder on the desk and walked into the living room.

Several of the day's early games were final or under way. Nick stretched out on the couch and studied the results and updates to see what influence, if any, they would have on his selections. Arizona destroyed Stanford, which made Nick suspicious of Southern Cal, who'd been blown out by the Cardinal two weeks ago and was catching eight points at Washington State. Maryland was up twenty at the half against Temple. This told Nick that Florida State, which had recently defeated the Terrapins, might be a solid play at home -10 versus Virginia.

After lying on the couch for an hour, Nick made his way back into the bedroom. He made two short entries in the folder, then charted the latest lines. There was much more movement this time around. Charlotte had fallen a half point to -11; Florida State had jumped a point to -11; and Vanderbilt, which was hosting SEC rival Florida, had dropped two points to -4. The Chicago Bulls and the University of Michigan were two exceptions. Their lines remained steady at -14.

Once he had the latest numbers charted, Nick leaned the folder against the desk and examined the first page. It was covered in red and black ink and contained information on ten college games, including an updated line from twelve different sports books. At the bottom of each column were notes that seemed coded so only Nick could interpret them. Injuries, which were scrawled in red, leapt from the page.

Nick flipped through the folder and studied the movement of each line. He then focused on the first number in each column and the last number, and calculated the difference between the two. If the remainder was three or more, it was circled. Using these forty-three numbers as a guide, he eliminated four games he was considering and added two to his list.

Shortly after 3 P.M., Nick double-clicked on the Sportsmaster icon and scanned for last-minute injuries and suspensions. Nothing was posted that he wasn't already aware of, so he slammed the folder shut. He then collected two pens from the desktop and rushed from the apartment.

Nick's first stop was at a drive-up ATM. He inserted his card into the machine and entered his pin number, 1973 (the year the Knicks last won the NBA championship). Withdrawal. From checking. $1,000. Please wait. Your transaction is being processed. . . . Insufficient funds. Would you like to make another transaction? Yes. Withdrawal. From checking. $900. Please wait. Your transaction is being processed. . . . Insufficient Funds. Yes. Withdrawal. Checking. $800. Please wait. Your transaction is being processed. . . .

After a brief pause, the machine made a low rumbling noise and dispensed eight hundred-dollar bills. Nick counted the money and after stuffing the bills in his back pocket, he glanced at the receipt. Balance: $11.27. Pulling away from the machine, he crumpled the receipt into a ball and flung it to the floorboard.

As usual on weekends, the Stardust's sports book was overrun with customers. In front of the expansive tote board, groups of men gathered, glanced up at the lines, then commented briefly to the person to their right or left. Directly behind them, the seating section was inundated with spectators; and every time a play was made on one of the overhead televisions, the crowd responded with approval and displeasure. Serpentine lines formed at the ticket windows. Men with line sheets curled in their hands looked up at the board as ticket writers handled the action. When someone stepped away from a window, the line pushed forward impatiently.

After collecting a line sheet from the counter, Nick found a seat at the back of the book and ordered a cocktail. He then set the sheet on top of his folder and began marking the latest line directly from the board. Chicago had gone up a half point to -14.5; Charlotte had leveled off at -11; and Florida State had ballooned to -11. Michigan, which Nick loved at home against Wisconsin, remained at -14. This pleased him. Sunset Station and the Reserve, two casinos close to his apartment, had the Wolverines at -14. Knowing the importance of a half point, Nick decided to make the longer drive to the Strip. He'd seen lives altered by a half point, and always tried to get the best line value available.

The waitress sidled down the row, balancing a tray of drinks. After collecting an empty beer bottle from the desk to Nick's right, she handed him a cocktail glass. He tipped her a dollar, stirred the drink, then yanked a stat sheet from the folder. Michigan was averaging 78.4 points a game and giving up 66.6. Wisconsin was averaging 60.4, while surrendering 62.8. Nick did some math on the top of the line sheet, then played the game in his head. He saw Michigan's big men catching the ball down low and scoring at will. He saw Michigan's guards draining three-pointers against a collapsing zone defense. He saw blocked shots, steals and easy baskets working in Michigan's favor. He saw a blowout. He reached into his back pocket and totaled his money. He had $1,310.

"Nicky, ya hit a big one or what?" inquired a baritone voice from the aisle. A heavyset man with silver hair and a flushed face started down the row.

Nick stuffed the money back in his pocket and smiled. "Need a big one, Sammy," he said. "Need a big one." The heavyset man drew near, extended his hand. "How's it going?" asked Nick, clasping it firmly.

"Not too well," admitted Sammy. He sat in the seat to Nick's right and, breathing heavily, explained, "Louisville killed me, the bastards. I had a three-teamer and the first two had already come in. All I needed was Louisville to cover six against goddamn DePaul, and they end up losing the game straight up. Cost me three hundred bucks. They gotta do something with Denny Crum. He's senile. They're down five with under a minute to go and he's not even pressing. It was unbelievable, Nicky. Unbelievable." Nick smiled, but didn't respond. "So how ya been?" asked Sammy.

"Not too bad," said Nick.

"You still at it?"

"Oh, yeah. Hangin' in there. Doing what I can. I moved the family out to Henderson four or five months back, so I don't make it out this way as much as I used to. Doing most of my work from the house now."

"Yeah? How's it going?"

"Not so good," Nick answered. "I've had one of the worst basketball seasons of my life, Sammy. It's been absolutely awful."

"You ain't the only one. Seems like everyone I've talked to has been gettin' killed. The books have made a fortune this season. An absolute killin'."

Nick shifted in his seat and glanced up at the board. "Ya like any of the late games, Sammy?"

Sam unrolled his line sheet and held it in front of him. "Think I'm gonna take a chance on Vandy. They've been playing pretty well lately, and they're always tough at home. Florida scares me, though. They've shown up at some really strange times this year." He paused, pulled the line sheet closer. "I also like U. Conn and West Virginia, but I don't know if I'm gonna put 'em in. That Louisville game hurt me bad, Nicky. I don't know if I'm gonna do anything else today."

"What do ya think about Michigan?" Nick inquired.

Sammy looked up at the board. "They should be able to cover fourteen, but they're a little too inconsistent for me. I still haven't gotten over that loss to Eastern Michigan. Haven't touched 'em since. Haven't even looked at 'em, to tell ya the truth."

Nick explained, "I'm not betting on Michigan as much as I'm betting against Wisconsin. They're awful this year. They've lost ten of their last eleven, and the one win they got was against a Division Two school."

"What's Michigan done lately?"

"They've won three of their last four. And in their last two games, they've looked really sharp. They beat Penn State by fifteen on the road and absolutely crushed Indiana at home."

"Yeah, I watched that Indiana game," said Sammy, disgustedly. "They looked like world beaters that night. The bastards can't cover seven against Eastern Michigan, but they beat Indiana by fifty. I can't make any sense of 'em, Nicky. Honestly, I can't."

Nick squinted at the clock on the far wall, then gathered his folder. "I gotta get something in before the bottom of the hour, Sammy," he said, rising.

"Okay, Nicky. Good to see ya. Good luck, all right."

"You too, Sammy. Take care of yourself."

Nick worked his way down the aisle and took a spot at the end of the shortest line. As he drew closer to the window, he surveyed the board to make sure he hadn't overlooked anything. He briefly reconsidered FSU, but again decided 11 was too many points. Villanova was tempting as well, with -2 at home, but he knew Rutgers had a much-improved ball club.

For the first time in eleven years of handicapping, Nick was visibly nervous. He stroked his goatee unconsciously, then ran his hand up and down the leg of his pants. Nothing on the board jumped out at him. It was as if the oddsmakers had set a perfect number on every game posted. He removed the line sheet from the folder and reviewed the games he'd circled: Arkansas vs. Alabama, Baylor vs. Texas A&M, Missouri vs. Kansas St., Michigan vs. Wisconsin. He reminded himself of all the research that went into each of the games. These aren't blind picks, he told himself. We're not just pulling teams out of hats here.

A man in a faded baseball cap walked away from the window. Nick stepped forward. "Give me one thirty for thirteen hundred dollars," he said.

"Michigan minus fourteen," confirmed the ticket writer, handing Nick the slip. Nick looked down at it and nodded. As his money was being filed in the drawer, he walked slowly away from the window.

It had been more than six months since Nick had watched an entire game in a sports book. He had a satellite dish at home and preferred the privacy of his living room, where he could listen to the commentary and follow the game without being disturbed. But on this day, he had no such luxury. The game was about to start and he didn't want to miss a single pass, shot, or steal. Plus, he was broke and needed to stick around to cash the ticket if Michigan covered.

After circling the book, Nick located an open chair near the back. And shortly after he was seated, the game tipped off. In the early going, things looked bad for Michigan. They turned the ball over repeatedly and missed several uncontested shots. At the first TV timeout, they trailed by five, 9–4. It was too early to panic, but it certainly wasn't the start Nick had envisioned. He shifted in his seat and watched some of the Arkansas/Alabama game. While waiting in line, he'd decided to go with Michigan instead of Arkansas because of the Razorbacks' poor road record against the spread. He was already beginning to regret this decision. Six minutes into the contest, Arkansas looked sharp and had a commanding 14–4 lead.

Wisconsin managed to stay close throughout the first half, mainly due to lackadaisical play on Michigan's part. The Wolverines continued to misfire on open shots and had several defense lapses, which led to easy buckets for the hustling Badgers. On a leaning three-pointer by point guard Jason Mason, Wisconsin led by one at the half, 31–30. Disgusted, Nick slammed the folder on the seat and stormed outside.

Nick had watched enough basketball in his life to realize he was in trouble. The flow of the game indicated Wisconsin would be competitive to the end, maybe even win the contest straight up. They were outshooting, outrebounding, and outhustling their more talented counterparts. There's no stat for desire, Nick concluded, tapping a cigarette from its pack and frisking for his lighter. There's nothing in your goddamn computer that can factor in how badly a team wants it.

He lit the cigarette, then violently removed his sports pager from his belt. He needed to see the halftime score again, just to confirm it was correct. Soon other updated scores followed: Texas 47 Colorado 43 H, Arkansas 37 Alabama 23 H, Missouri 16 Kansas St. 6 1st H 14:31. . . .

After watching his pager for a full rotation, Nick felt nauseous. Three of the four other teams he'd considered looked strong and were on track to cover. If he'd only split the money between the teams, as he customarily did, he would've been in relatively good shape. But as it was, he was handcuffed. All of his money was tied into one game; he didn't have a single cent to work with. All he had in his wallet was the Michigan ticket—and he would've traded that in for half of what he paid for it if it was possible.

Michigan played much better in the second half. The game Nick envisioned finally began to materialize on the court. The Wolverines pounded the ball down low and scored or got to the free throw line and converted. When Wisconsin's defense collapsed, Michigan's guards got good looks at the basket and knocked down the open three. With just under ten minutes remaining, Michigan seized momentum and led by six, 49–43. For the first time all game, Nick had reason to be optimistic.

But Wisconsin hung tough. They were a much better club than their record and statistics indicated. They fell on loose balls, played unselfishly, and had an experienced, hard-nosed backcourt. Every time Michigan threatened to blow the game open, Wisconsin responded with a big play. And with three minutes remaining, the Badgers trailed by only two and had possession of the ball.

Nick needed a miracle. Even if Michigan maintained the lead and made free throws down the stretch, it was unlikely they'd cover the fourteen-point spread. As the final seconds ticked away, he retrieved his folder and headed for the exit. When the final score flashed across the screen—Michigan 76 Wisconsin 70—he'd already traversed the parking lot and climbed into his car.

After allowing a stream of pedestrians to pass, Nick turned onto the Strip. The sidewalks were lined with tourists and the lanes chocked full of charter buses and rental cars. The gridlock didn't appear to frustrate Nick. In fact, he seemed more comfortable when his car was idling than lurching forward. He was traveling south, but had no particular destination.

After making a left-hand turn onto Tropicana Avenue, he adjusted the rearview mirror and observed the western horizon. The sun had dropped behind the mountains, silhouetting the flat peaks and small hills stationed at their base. Shaded, the range looked like rolling waves that were destined to crash onto the condos to the west and flood the Las Vegas Valley. He readjusted the mirror and accelerated.

Easy Driving

THOMAS A. PORTER

Today was supposed to have been one of the greatest days of my life. Supposed to have been.

What was supposed to have happened was this: I was going to drive from Vegas to San Francisco, and somewhere on that drive, somewhere between Las Vegas and San Francisco, I was supposed to hit the big 100,000-mile mark.

That would have been a record. More than that—it would have been *the* record. No one even knows what the old record is, which is kinda weird. But still, everyone I ask sure as hell admits that 100,000 miles is a new one. Hell, not many people can stay at this job long enough to get *half* that many miles in. I should know. I been here longer than anyone. Sometimes it seems like I been doing this forever.

Just not that many people can stick it out and make it work for them—it takes a special kind of guy. What I do is "redistribute moveable corporate assets." That's kind of my big way of saying it. What that means is that I drive rental cars, from one city to another. I work for the Sunshine Agency, and they arrange to get cars from where people leave them to where people want them. Say, for example, everyone all a sudden decides that the best vacation going is the drive from New York to Florida. Well, then, either someone has to convince people that Florida to New York is just as good a drive, get them to drive them back and pay for the privilege, or they have to pay me to get the cars back to New York before Florida gets even more jammed up with cars than it already is.

I'll drive anywhere—it's not a vacation for me. It's what I do. I'm always moving, always on the go. In the past six months I've been all over the country. It's like this: one day I'll take a full-size luxury car to one place, Boston, say. Then from there a different company needs a subcompact driven back to D.C., and then maybe a midsize to Philly, and on and on and on. Sometimes I'll get stuck somewhere for a day or two, but that's okay. It doesn't happen very often. There always seems to be a car that needs to get somewhere. Sometimes I'll drive identical cars, same make, same model, back and forth between cities but for different companies. Go figure. Sunshine picks up my meals, pays for the motel rooms, and I get fifty bucks a day and four cents a mile. The mileage is where the money adds up—longer drives, more money, not that that matters as much as you might think it does.

What *does* matter, more and more the longer I've been doing this, is the record, that 100,000 miles. The money? I stopped even cashing my paychecks awhile back—I just cash one every now and then, when I need walking-around money. I've got all the other checks, five months' worth almost, in an envelope in the bottom of my gym bag.

I've got everything in that bag. There's the checks, my shaving bag and stuff, enough underwear and socks for ten days. The same with T-shirts and sweat pants. I drive in loose clothes—otherwise they bind up on you. I've got a button-down shirt and a pair of khakis for when I need to dress up, and I can get everything into one washing machine and be in and out of a Laundromat in under an hour. No lost time. Besides the clothes and stuff I've got a lumbar pillow I bought at a gift shop near Tucson, a stainless-steel coffee mug from a truck stop outside of Dallas, and a thermos.

And I've got the tape, too. Somewhere back I found this tape in one of the cars. It's called *How to Win Friends and Influence People,* and I swear I have it about memorized by now. I've never heard of anything like this tape. It just *gives* you the secrets for dealing with people, and the stuff *works.* For example, when I meet people now, I look them right in the eyes when I shake their hands, and I don't squeeze too hard or hang on too long, either. Another thing is I don't show my teeth when I smile—that's threatening to some folks. I really work at remembering names, even if I know I'll never see someone again. Little things like that. The tape is just full of little things I'd never even thought of, the kinds of things that might make a difference one day. You never know.

I got the idea from the tape of having the *goal.* Not the number—100,000—but the idea of setting myself a mark, a pretty high mark at that, and then shooting for it. That's what the tape calls "self-driven motivation." And it works. Once I had the goal—oh, awhile back now—once I had it to look forward to, the days just started to fall away, one after another, and the miles really started to pile up. It's important, to work toward something, to see it working out, the planning and everything.

I'm pretty careful about keeping track of my miles. For the company, sure, for the money, but more and more, the closer I get, for the *goal*. My last few days were Denver to Albuquerque, 439 miles. Albuquerque to Tucson, 452. And yesterday, Tucson to Vegas, 407 miles. 100,000 miles—that's something. It really is.

Today, when I woke up in Vegas, at a motel on Fremont Street, my head was pounding. It was so full that I could hear my heartbeat, like someone pounding a drum in the next room—*thub, thub, thub*. I mean I had a *headache*. A bad one, the kind I get sometimes from driving with the sun in my eyes all day. I just lay there for a while with my eyes closed and I didn't even want to move enough to shut off the alarm. I swear I could feel whatever was clogging me up sliding around in my head, all thick and sticky, like tar or something.

I knew right away what had happened. Driving with the air conditioner on and the windows up'll give me a head cold every time. But what could I have done? All the way from Tucson in that crappy little compact. Almost nine hours of hot, dry desert and the air conditioner could only just keep it cool enough to breathe without hurting. Damn.

I pulled on a pair of sweats and a T-shirt and went out and got some eardrops and cold pills from the 7-Eleven on the corner. When I got back in the room, I used the bathroom mirror to put in the drops—I have to look or I miss. I worked them down in there with my fingers, rubbing behind my ears and working my jaw around, but nothing came clear.

I thought about how, if I had still been with Mary, if I'd been at home, she'd have warmed up a little oil in a saucepan and used a cotton ball to drip it in my ear, and I'd have sat with my head on the kitchen table for a minute while it melted through whatever was in there. I would have sat there until it cooled and then I'd have held a paper towel against my head and turned over and the oil would have run out and then everything would have cleared right up.

But I wasn't with Mary anymore, and I wasn't at home. I was in a bathroom in a motel in Vegas. That's the way life is. You just have to keep getting up in the morning, no matter what. I kept thinking about all of that while I showered and got dressed again, and I knew it was right. You have to keep going, keep looking ahead. Looking back is like trying to drive a car by looking out the back window at where you've been instead of forward, at where you're going. I knew where I was going—I was hitting the record books today—and even with the run to the store I still made it out the door half an hour after my alarm. That's another thing I learned from the tape. If you set yourself a schedule, stick to it.

On my way to the car, I had to walk around this scummy swimming pool. The water was dark green, like soup. I had a thought that maybe it was that that had stuffed me up and not the driving yesterday. Last night when I checked in it had smelled like Florida, down in the Everglades, all warm and gassy. When I'd opened the door to my room the air in there was just full of that stink. I tried to smell it again as I walked by the pool, but all I got was a weird noise, a honking sound like a goose.

I was driving a new red Buick Skylark, for Avis. Nice car. Sunroof, electric everything, cruise control. Only seven thousand miles on it. The tank had been full when I'd picked it up last night, so it was ready to roll. I got in, wrote down the time and the mileage in my book and figured out how many more miles I needed for the record, for about the hundredth time, I'd say. Then I drove back down to the 7-Eleven and filled my coffee cup and thermos. I jumped on Interstate 15 south, and by the time the sun was all the way up and the heat got really bad, I was already three hours across the desert, almost out of it, just like I'd planned on.

All morning I kept working my jaws back and forth, up and down, trying to get something to shift in there. I tried plugging my nose with my fingers, again and again, puffing out my cheeks like a trumpet player. Nothing doing—I was blocked tight.

After three hours I pulled over at a rest stop outside of Bakersfield. I was careful about my breaks and always took them, no matter how many miles I had to go in a day. Fifteen minutes for morning and afternoon break, a half hour for lunch. If I drove more than eight hours in a day I'd add breaks when I felt like it, but I liked to keep my days down to eight hours. You had to if you wanted to keep doing this job day in, day out. I took a piss, washed a couple of cold pills down and then I did my stretches—knee bends, toe touches, and shoulder swings. Fifteen each. When I bent to touch my toes I thought my head was going to explode, but I did them anyway. If I didn't, by the time I got to San Francisco I knew I'd be too stiff to walk, let alone make it down to the coffee shop. It was going to be a long day—577 miles. At *least* eleven hours and that was if I pushed it a little.

The heat was still pretty bad, and my shirt was wet through by the time my break was over. The waves shimmering up off the road made the big trucks appear out of nowhere, like out of a fog bank. God, it was hot, but I still took my full fifteen minutes. I half hoped that the sun might bake something dry in my head, but nothing happened except that when I started driving again my headache was even worse.

By the time I stopped for lunch, my head was really throbbing. My ears felt like they were stuffed full of hot sand, and my nose was packed solid. I could hear myself wheezing every time I took a breath. I was in pretty sorry shape. I popped a couple more pills and tried the drops again while I washed up for lunch, and the whole time I was sitting at the table I tried to work something free, massaging behind my ears with my fingers. All that did for me was make my neck feel bruised back there from pressing so hard.

Outside again it was hot—over a hundred easy. I stood in the shade for a second, picking at my teeth with a toothpick, and then I started to walk over to the car. As I walked I took the toothpick and slid it down in my ear. I could feel something in there, something hard, and I thought about what I used to tell my kids when they were little to keep them from sticking things in their ears. I thought of a bean growing in there, or a rock stuck forever, but it felt so good. It felt like I was just about to pop something and let the pressure out. My hand was shaking a little, and I could feel the end of the toothpick kind of scraping along in there, and I went a little deeper—it was just such an "almost" kind of feeling. I had my eyes closed and I went up on tiptoe, and I was concentrating on the tip of that toothpick way down deep in my head when the hitchhiker popped out of nowhere.

"You heading north?"

I must have jumped a mile.

"Jesus," I yelled, "I almost stuck this right in my ear!" I waved it at him for a second and then caught sight of myself and dropped my hand down, like he'd caught me picking my nose or something.

"Sorry," I said. "You just startled me." I smiled and held out my hand. The tape said if you put it out there, they'd take it. Sure enough, after a second the kid did. Right away my head felt a little bit better. Something about having a person around always seems to make me feel good, and just standing there and shaking the kid's hand did something for me.

I gave him a quick, firm shake, one-two, and then stepped back. The guy was young, maybe eighteen, twenty, somewhere in there, thin, clean-cut. He wore worn hiking boots and jeans, a new Hooters T-shirt, and he had a dusty duffel bag leaning back against his legs.

"You looking for a ride?" I said, and when I realized I still had the toothpick in my hand I dropped it behind my leg. "I'm heading to San Francisco."

That's the only company rule I ever broke, the one about hitch-hikers. I didn't smoke or eat in the cars, never just parked them somewhere and walked away. I didn't use them for personal er-rands, nothing like that. But I always picked up hitchhikers. Some-times I'd have two or three at once and I just loved to listen to their stories. It made the days pass quicker, being involved with people like that. My notebook was full of addresses from all over the coun-try. Overseas, too. New York, Seattle, Europe, Australia.

"San Fran where you're heading?" I asked him.

"Yeah." The kid smiled, kind of distantlike, but he seemed friendly. I'd become a pretty good judge of character. "That'd be perfect."

"Brian Phelps." I almost reached out to shake the kid's hand again. "You a student up there?" I wanted to make the kid relax after my having yelled at him like that. He'd really startled me there.

"I'm trying to get to my sister's in San Francisco."

I got the keys out and popped the trunk.

"Well, hey. This is your lucky day, then," I said.

The kid lifted his bag and shuffled toward me. I could see that the bag was heavy by the way he moved, and when he dropped it in the trunk, the car settled lower into its springs.

"You've got a lot of stuff," I said as I walked around and unlocked the driver's door. I checked my watch to make sure my lunch hour was over and then got in. It took me a second to find the button to unlock the doors. It's in a different place in every car, I swear.

When the kid got in, I pointed at my gym bag on the back seat. "Not me. I travel light. What do you need a whole bunch of stuff for, right?"

The kid just sat there, hands on his knees, facing forward. A little spacey but harmless.

"Buckle up," I said. I always wore mine, and I made everyone else too—I'd have hated to be driving a car full of hitchhikers *without* their seat belts on, God forbid something ever happened. While the kid did himself up, I filled my cup out of my thermos and dropped the thermos behind my seat. I kept talking, wanting to get the kid to relax a little bit. His just sitting there like that was a little awkward.

"You have to wait long for a ride?"

"No, not really." The kid's voice was soft, and I snuck another peek at him. He hadn't moved once he got his belt on, hands on his knees, eyes half closed. Harmless, though. Maybe a little nervous about me, because I had yelled at him, maybe just tired, maybe even stoned—but harmless. What the hell, right? It was too late to start worrying now. No sense looking back.

I set the cruise control, cracked a back window, and got my pillow settled down behind my back.

"Sixty-seven miles an hour," I said. "Any more and they pull you over, any less and you get passed like you're standing still." Still nothing, so I figured I'd hold it awhile.

I stared out at the road. I love this part of the country. It's all flat and straight, nothing on either side of the road but fields. The farms must be huge because there seems to be forever between turnoffs, and it's an easy stretch to drive. There's not much lane changing going on, everyone in the middle of getting from one place to another. It's harder to drive when there are lots of people jumping on and off the highway all the time, changing lanes, speeding up, slowing down. But like this, everyone heading somewhere a couple of hours away, it's nice and smooth. Easy driving.

After a while, I started to talk to the kid again.

"I'm a driver," I said. "This is what I do." I took a sip of coffee and set the cup down between my thighs, and waved my hand out at the fields and the road. "It's not a bad job, let me tell you."

I looked over again, but the kid just sat there, hand on his knees, nodding like the radio was on.

"This isn't even my car." That got a little bit of a reaction. He at least turned his head. I could feel my head clearing, and I rolled my shoulders a little and twisted my neck, and the stiffness there was going, too.

"It's not stolen, if that's what you're thinking. I'm a driver, for the rental car companies, and I need forty—" I looked down and waited for a number to click over—"forty-*one* more miles before I'll have the company record."

I took another sip of coffee.

"The most miles ever." I looked over at him, waiting to see a reaction—but nothing. He just sat there, looking straight ahead, like he didn't even care where he was going. It was a little weird.

"That's a record. But it's more than that, though, more than the driving."

The words flowed out and we both just stared straight ahead at the road. I kept talking, and I almost forgot the kid was even there, he was so quiet. I told him about the goal, about what that meant to me, and then I told him other things, too. I told him about the first time I had ever kissed Mary, about how her breath had smelled like trees, how warm the skin of her face had felt against my cheek. I talked about getting married, so long ago I sometimes felt like it was a memory from someone else's life, or something I'd seen in a movie. I talked about my kids, where I thought they were, what they'd been doing the last time I'd spoken to them on the phone, and I told him about how I sort of woke up one day and realized I was divorced and Mary was married to someone else. I was still not quite sure how all that had happened. It had just seemed to creep up on me, on us, I guess. Never saw it coming, and then one day there it was.

"Almost ten years," I said, "and then one day I came home and Mary asked me to leave. And I did. Just like that. I can't even remember why now, or how it was such an easy thing to do—but I just *left*." I almost whispered that last word, and I remember moving my hand, waving it like I was tossing something, a gum wrapper or a piece of trash, down on the floor. "I just *left*. And pretty soon after that I quit my job and moved, and then I moved again, and then I took a job in Chicago, and then in Memphis, and then somewhere else and I can't hardly believe it's all so long ago now. Where did the time go?"

I looked down then and saw that I was getting close. While I'd been talking the miles had been falling away, down to thirty, then twenty, then fifteen, ten, without me noticing, but we were close now. I switched off the cruise control and slowed down.

"You still with me, kid?" I reached out and touched him on the knee, and he jerked his head like I'd stabbed him with a pencil.

"One Hundred Thousand Miles," I said, feeling myself getting excited. "Coming up."

"Why're you slowing down?" There was a panic in his voice that threw me for a second.

"Hey—no," I said, "nothing like that. I just want to get a picture, maybe scoop up some dirt, get a souvenir. . . ." I heard myself and knew he thought I was nuts, stopping by the side of the road like that, but he didn't understand about the goal, about how important it was.

I was still slowing down, edging over to the shoulder where the road just sort of fell away, steeply, down to the cleared fields. A car honked as it passed us.

"Look," I said, "I know it's a little bit much, but would you take a picture? I have a camera. . . ."

I reached back for my bag and swung it over into my lap, and that was it. The bag hit my coffee cup, and I felt the coffee spill across my legs, and when I looked down it was pouring out onto the leather.

"Shit!"

I arched myself back, and the bag kind of jumped off my lap and landed up on the dash, tangled in the wheel. I tried to grab it with my other hand, and then I heard the kid scream, there was a loud noise, and everything went dark.

When I opened my eyes, I was hanging upside down. I shook my head, trying to get my eyes to focus, but the air seemed to be full of dust or something. I heard a thud and a scrabbling sound and turned my head in time to see the kid crawling out where his window would have been if it hadn't broken into a thousand pieces. The top of the car under my head was covered in glass, and my coffee cup lay on its side next to the overhead light in the middle of a big coffee stain. Then my door jerked open, and the kid's face was there, upside down, sweaty and panicked looking.

"You okay?" he asked me, and I could hear him breathing, hard.

"Huh?" I said. Something was wrong—I knew that much but I couldn't get anything to focus.

"We rolled," the kid said again. "We rolled off the shoulder." He was breathing so hard he was almost sobbing. I looked at his face, still upside down, and then it was like someone had thrown a switch. Everything straightened out. I knew what had happened. I'd gone off the road.

"Jesus," I said. "We rolled?" The kid leaned in under me, and I felt his fingers digging at the buckle to my seat belt, and when it gave, I half fell on top of him, my legs still knotted up under the dash. He crawled out, backward, and I tried to use my hands and feet to help, and once we were a few feet away from the car I sort of rolled off of him and lay on my back. The kid turned around and knelt right by my head, and his hands were dancing around, fluttering next to my face like panicked birds, but they never touched me.

"We rolled?" I said again. I was trying to get it straight, but my head was still pretty woozy and nothing wanted to stay still for very long. I wanted to ask the kid to sit back and let me catch my breath for a second and figure out what had happened, but he was sweating and breathing hard, like he'd just run a really fast mile or something.

"Listen," he said to me, "I'll run up to the road and stop someone. Just lay here, okay?"

Wait, I wanted to say, but before I could he was gone and I was staring up at the bright blue sky where his face had been. I half heard the sound of his boots scurrying in the sand, and then that sound faded, and it was quiet except for the ticking sound that the engine made as it cooled down.

I groaned and sat up. I wanted to see better, but sitting up made my head spin, and I leaned to the side and vomited. Lunch came up, and I heaved again, and then right away I felt better, like it had been something that I needed to do. I wiped my mouth on my hand and got some sand in my teeth, and then I looked at the car.

It was upside down, its top smashed in pretty good, all the windows gone, and its front end was half buried in the sand. I could smell antifreeze and gas. The driver's door was open, and on the headliner my gym bag and coffee cup were surrounded by shiny bits of glass. I stared at it for a minute, and then I rolled over and got on my hands and knees, and this made my head spin again. I thought I was going to be sick but after a second it passed and I started to crawl over to the car. When I got my head inside it was so dark all of a sudden that I couldn't see anything but little dancing spots for a second. I closed my eyes, tight, and that pitching feeling started to get worse, but when I opened my eyes again it went away.

I craned my neck around and looked up. The gas and brake pedals were still in their right places, the steering wheel was there, and it looked like the car was ready to just drive away. I turned over on my back, slowly, and rested my head on my gym bag. It was comfortable enough. I could feel my coffee cup digging into one of my shoulders, and there were bits of glass pressing sharp into my back.

I reached up and grabbed the steering wheel with both hands, and used it to pull myself up. When I was almost sitting up straight, I felt hands on my legs and reaching in around my waist.

"Whoa," I heard someone say. Not the kid—someone else. Hands came and took hold of my wrists.

"Whoa. You ain't going anywheres right now, son."

I squeezed my eyes closed again, and everything started to tilt and rock. My hands opened and I felt myself drawn out of the car and half carried, half dragged a few feet, and then I was let down on the hot sand. I lifted my arm and dropped it down over my eyes, and there seemed to be a great many voices now. The sand was warm under me, and I almost felt as if I might fall asleep there. I lay listening, and after a while I felt myself lifted, hands at my waist and shoulders and under my legs, and as they carried me I could hear, as if from far away, the sound of breathing and the scuffle of feet in sand, and the faint ticking sound of the engine cooling down in the hot desert sun.

Mr. Biondi and the
New Dispensation

GERMAN SANTANILLA

Mr. Biondi looked out of the tent into the parking lot mess, the hundreds of cowboy types and their jeans-clad women, boots of all kinds of leather, hats of all materials deemed suitable for Western attire. This would be a fine place for a murder. The uniform clothes, the uniform physiques, the beer and the glare, the noise and the heat would all compensate for whatever flaws the planned entertainment might have.

Although, Mr. Biondi mused, "entertainment" was not the most felicitous term for such an art form. He had been up nights trying to think of a more formally correct name for such impromptu stagings, the arting of violence in discrete steps, the deconstruction of public peace and complacency into a more satisfying social space in which to live. The infusing of an element of art, of drama, into everyday existence was, he held, a desideratum of urban planning, and if his former associates at the old Committee for Public Safety didn't quite agree with his methods, that just went to show how far back they had fallen from their glorious heights as the town's only anarcho-syndicalist art collective.

His plan was to analyze the noise content in the medium of urban violence, in order to arrive at a method that would let him predict where and when a crime would be so likely that it would get lost in the background noise, so that a murder would barely rise above this noninformation; the stagings would be lightninglike, impromptu, old-fashioned guerrilla theater. This was the birth of BETA, Biondi's Experimental Theater Artists, and its more public, proactive branch, its more mathematically themed offshoot, NOISE. A regression analysis had revealed that a crime of passion and violence was quite likely to occur at a public gathering of this sort; no extra security or police protection had been assigned to this tent sale and rodeo. A couple arguing, too much beer, a man walking away in a huff, a few shots from smoking Colt .45s, squealing tires, and the screams of the abduction victim, all surreally arranged to provide the police with several believable but mutually contradictory clues; this was a well-planned work of art.

The first BETA project had gone somewhat awry when a real gang-banger drive-by wounded the first intended "victim," a fellow member of NOISE, a slam poet called Jack. This had taught NOISE to be more careful about the type of crime they would parody: a carjacking or drive-by in Rollin' Westies turf would likely not be attempted again. Next, a rehearsal kidnapping of an Asian tourist had been a howling success: headlines about the SAHEL CASINO KIDNAPPING had blared for the requisite two and a half days as measured in local press units by a cynical NOISE member who critiqued the media in an "alternative" paper. A carful of racially mixed terrorists (dressed in the most offensively stereotyped clothing one could imagine outside of Charlie Chan and Fu Manchu movie serials) had pulled up alongside the hotel parking lot and the festively dressed thugs jumped out, clubbed their hapless victim, who shouted for justice and vengeance to the heavens in Japanese, threw him in a sack, and laughing toothy Tojo laughter, made off with him. The air of unreality in the parking lot of the hotel was to become a trademark of the BETA and NOISE capers. The witnesses' descriptions, some of which were not made up or planted, were so astounding and full of discrepancies that the police all but gave up. The candidate for sheriff of the New Dispensation Party, a local political alliance, used it to accuse the current officeholder of ruining the tourist trade by being soft on crime.

The next rehearsal had happened the week of the implosion of the old Icehouse, when the last rave was held in the stripped and gutted building. The recording of *Ambient Masterpieces: Music for Cheap Synthesizer, Guitar, and Tuba* (the last work commissioned by the old committee acting as the Ton-Kluster Sozietät for reasons best known only to its Viennese members) was followed by a Vampyre Rave, which was crashed by masked members of NOISE, who rushed the stage and ritually impaled Vladimir F., the sci-fi novelist, and ran off giggling into the desert night; the next day the imploding building hid any traces of the simulacrum, and given the overabundance of smart drinks and the attendant glut of detailed eyewitness descriptions, no sense was ever made of the night's events. The only clue was an engraved calling card, left by the Chevalier de Saint Denis, the Prior of Nôtre Dame. However, it happened to be the real thing, and caused the Cross and the Rose a deal of explaining at the District Court Occult Division.

The Eighth Judicial District Court had lately elevated the Occult Division to full State Superior Court level, complete with a Discovery commission and bench and jury trials. Its presiding judge, a proper Presbyterian, sat uncomfortably in his robes, state and national flags at his back, between icons of Metatron and Changó, hoping that no members of his congregation would ever have reason to come to his courtroom; he still felt that, though the Occult Division had a legitimate function, some of its trappings and, well, rituals, might cause a little discomfort with the more sedate, more traditional Christians in town. The origins of this division of the court system went back a few years, to the infamous "Chicken Patrol," whose function was, at first, to clean up the dead chickens and the bird entrails left at a corner of the old jail by some defendants' families as sacrifice, religious observance, or plain old intimidation. The duties of the patrol grew to the investigation of occult threats away from the detention center, and then into the full-blown study of Santería, Voudoun, Kabbalah, Umbanda, Candomblé, Illuminism, Enochian Great Work, and all sorts of other esoteric doctrines favored by local ethnic gangs.

After some complex Ninth Circuit decisions in the case of *Estate of John Dee v. O. T. O. Nevada,* the division was formed by the District Attorney's Office; the court appointed a hearing master and began hearing civil complaints and ruling on disputes of a less criminal matter, growing to its present power, which had competence over the controversies arising within and between several esoteric, nativistic, and traditional belief structures. The presiding judge, not only a Mason but a Presbyterian elder and a corresponding member of the Skeptic Council of North America, suffered a lot of nonsense in his post, but, hey, it was better than juvenile court. Or at least more interesting.

Today's kidnapping was itself a rehearsal for a more elaborate staging, a simulacrum of a murder, something juicy that would shake up the town, something with political implications that would wipe out the usual front-page fodder of election scandals, nepotism charges, pictures of well-known license plates at hot-sheet motels and the like, the diversion of Western small-town Big Fun. The bourgeoisie needed awakening, and NOISE was to be the alarm bell. The world is dangerous! You are not safe, not even here in the midst of the sagebrush and neon.

A peculiarity of the desert landscape is that in the clear, dry air, objects appear closer than they really are. The fact that this is not explained on any warning stickers, like the one on your sideview mirrors, explains a lot about your Johnny-come-lately desert rat. South of the E-Z Lay Motel, away from the encroaching city lights, a hiker may be excused for trying to walk to the next line of hills, underestimating the distance by a factor of ten. So it may happen that a couple of rookies from KC may err in heading off the dirt road they travel to tote a long, suspicious bundle carrying the body of someone with a nickname like "the Chin," or "Little Can," and wind up paying their respects to the departed warrior in a very Mesopotamian way, to be eventually covered by alluvial sands.

Such a random dotting of bodies in the desert outskirts comes to light after a good rainy summer, and any bones whatever, as long as they are found in vaguely similar contexts, such as washes, near caves or mines, become ipso facto the bones of any recently missing person. The overworked but somehow still humorous forensic anthropologist, who had been the sole examiner of such finds for years, kept a roomful of "suspected human remains" in her garage for the instruction of her students. Only lions and tigers were missing from the menagerie, which included otherwise camelids, canids, ursids, and horses. The local police had recently emerged from the Dark Ages in this respect and now hardly ever took unarticulated long bones to the professor without long and perspicacious debate as to the possible humanity of the donor.

The local custom of seeding the desert floor with stiffs was ripe for parody, an opportunity that the old CPS and its spin-offs, BETA and NOISE (which now left its logo, an eye in the screen of a stylized oscilloscope, everywhere), did not let pass. Starting with theatrical props and medical model leftovers from syndicated "reality TV" shows, and with assorted suburban debris, a series of human-sacrifice-remains sites were artfully created and set up in corners of the valley that were physically distant or of difficult access but frequented by skateboarders, hikers, dirt bike riders, illicit concert producers, and, of course, wanna-be death metal human sacrifice cultists. The props were as quickly and artfully removed before the police ever arrived; and by now, with the increasing frequency of reports of ritually-disposed-of human remains, alien mutilations, and satanic kidnappings that mostly turned out to be the urban desert equivalent of swamp gas, the potential ethnic violence and rumored political murders that the New Dispensation Party election posters promised appeared in the distance ahead on the blacktop and then melted like shimmering summer mirages.

Then there was the matter of the Naked Guy; its minimalist logo adorned flyers and posters yearly, beginning around May Day. Artists and anarchists prepared themselves by buying and processing chemicals. Musicians built new and wondrous instruments and composed tortuous rhythm cycles based on Fibonacci series, Carnatic talas, and Gamelan percussion counterpoint and melodic modules. Sculptors designed giant cocktail glasses and erotic candelabra. Poets drank themselves giddy and attempted to write Naked Guy poetry, and for a while slams around town got a little weird.

The Original Naked Guy had moved to town from Mission Viejo years ago with a vision: an effigy somewhat like himself, several stories tall, and definitely, absolutely male, burning at dawn on the longest day of the year on a dry lake. Originally, there was to be an atmospheric nuke test as a background, but it was difficult to arrange and the Naked Guy was briefly held on suspicion of nuclear terrorism.

Later, as the sixties wore on into the seventies, the eighties, and then worse, it became a more apolitical, anarchic ritual with no discernible purpose, but with a powerful, primal glamour that melded punk, metalhead, industrial, and folkie sensibilities, that combined artisans, mechanics, media-savvy voyeurs, cyber voyants, and tribal voyageurs into a naked, writhing mass of sweating performance. The sixties Happening was not dead here; as purified and reconstituted, filtered through arena concerts, the electroacoustic

environmental Pied Piper pieces of Terry Riley, the drumming circles of Deadheads, and some vague trend in the Western psyche
that surfaced variously as tribal, trance, and rave, it lived, it danced,
like some corporate Golem, with the name of an unknown god in its
mouth, and the word EMET glowing on its sweaty forehead. The
Guy would be accompanied in its journey to oblivion by the Giant
Martini, the Exploding National Landmarks, the re-creation of
some aptly chosen catastrophe, such as the Big Bang, and a train-
load of mini Happenings, like the nude-and-ludicrous tableaux of
historical events, great battles, literary scenes, great sculptures
and paintings; the Penis Envy contest, featuring hundreds of quite
artistic strap-ons, displayed in priapic splendor and thought by
the faithful to appease the well-endowed effigy; the snake dances,
the drum circles carrying the whole-tone-blues-over-an-Enigmatic-
Scale-bass that was the musical theme of the festival (a low, slow
thrum that still haunts and thrills some ears); the drawing of Nazca
lines; the alien abductions, which may not all have been due to the
ever-present smart drinks; the visit of the Green Man; the Corn
Mother Ritual, and the small-scale weirdnesses to which bohemian
flesh is heir. The ultimate aim of the Naked Guy—the person, not
the effigy—was to build a 1:1 scale model of the Strip and implode
the mother.

The New Dispensation Party, a local political alliance, hoped to
make election-year hay out of the Naked Guy. The NDP, a squeaky-
clean outfit, stood foursquare for what the city stood for: sin, sex,
and drink, in their rightful places. That is, as commodities that sold
seats, filled rooms, and fed slot machines. Outside of that, nudity,
drunkenness, and frolics were to be stringently regulated, if at all
allowed.

Through all of this, the Naked Guy traveled impassive, like a
Plains Sioux chief, like a Sudhee, his mind taken up by visions of
the 38-foot-tall effigy, manly and proud, burning at dawn on the
summer solstice, amid the tribal rejoicing of a few thousand brave
celebrants. The NDP had put forth a Position Paper, in which the
Naked Guy, among other local causes célèbres, was reviled as yet
another blotch on the city's family-friendly image, its hordes of
nude hippies disporting in body-painted, Saturnalian abandon, one
more sure sign of just where Civilization was headed. The titular

head of the NDP (the real power behind it being a mysterious figure combining the features of El Tapado, El Maximón, and the Mahdi), the son of a movie cowboy and an early talkies sex symbol, hinted that the Guy was one of many things that would be put to rights when the NDP achieved its destiny: no more bonfire-lit skatedeboardin' punk-filled rockin' good times at the edge of town, no more public money for the junk passed off as art by greasy hipsters, no more free rides for the fringe element.

It may be true that this was the root of the enmity between BETA and NOISE, the Jacobins of the committee, and the NDP; the anarchist wing of the local arty crowd lost no chance to ridicule the political posturing of NDP candidates; underground 'zines and free papers were filled with scathing editorials and vicious cartoons featuring the movie cowboy and his pals. I must state, in the interest of objective journalism, that this was hardly the only source of friction between the NDP and the Jacobins: their street theater and guerrilla performance art irritated the thin-skinned political establishment that was trying to pass off this overgrown truck stop of a town as the Family Entertainment Mecca of the World.

And now, with the coming of summer and the Naked Guy frenzy, Mr. B's guerrilla stagings of simulated crimes had reached a crescendo. The drive-by shooting of the poet, the impaling of Vladimir at the Vampyre rave, the kidnapping of the Japanese tourist, the infamous and almost perfect shoot-out at the rodeo, with its pretentious allusions to Shakespeare, John Ford, and Kurosawa, the frequent sightings of hermetic ritual sacrifice victims whose bodies appeared to vanish at the mere mention of the authorities— all seemed to point to some greatness ahead, a truly monumental crime, something that would wake up the city, excite the populace; and perhaps, just perhaps the Naked Guy would provide the next stage for this public Grand Guignol.

Golfers

DAVID SCOTT

Earnie and Sandov sat on the Champions' Bench outside the pro shop. The flower boxes siding the first tee had sprouted new color after last night's storm, with petunias, marigolds, poppies, and snapdragons invading each other's space. The rainy smell of desert sage still lingered in the drying air. Down the fairway, the lake nudged the high-water marks on the bridges stitching the gash that the water tore through the first and eighteenth fairways. Pines and oaks maintained the borders between the fairways and hid the rest of the course from view. In the distance, Mount Charleston rose from a dry brown cloud and sealed the course in a greenhouse of peace.

The sun blazed high over the two men; the shadow from the roof cut across their knees, keeping most of their bodies cool, but their polyester slacks and their old leather golf shoes warmed their shins and feet. Their checkered, short-sleeved shirts swelled as they breathed, the skin of their tanned arms sagged around the elbows, and their hands, calloused in the palms, rested in their laps. Equally bushy silver hair softened the edges of Sandov's hatchet face and sharp nose and sharpened Earnie's round cheeks and bulbous nose. Sandov lifted a hand to scratch his left elbow. He hated the violent weather extremes in the spring, the constant change from storm to dry, hot wind always bothering his skin. Earnie had his head tilted against the pro shop's front wall and his blue fisherman's cap pulled over his eyes as if he were asleep, but his eyes flickered after the foursome of ladies on the first tee, the brawny young man at the table to their left, the busboy from the country club bringing a sandwich to the starter's booth, the little kids leaving their golf lesson, bouncing green balls on the asphalt and twirling their putters like batons as they scurried from the putting green beyond the shop.

Earnie and Sandov had arrived in Las Vegas in the late forties, moving from course to course, outward from the Strip as the city had grown. Fifteen years ago, they had given up trying to outrun the city and the ridiculously high greens fees that had followed. They had found this course a week after it opened and had settled here. Tucked away in an upscale neighborhood, this course still had its quiet days—remote from the crowd on the Strip, a tough maze of par threes and par fours that swallowed hooks in the lake and slices in the neighborhood yards. They had learned how to play the middle way on this course. Swing easy, hit straight, watch the big hitters trap themselves in the water hazards and bunkers and backyards waiting for them. Earnie and Sandov did not have their names on the Champions' Bench (the winners of the club tournament each year had their names engraved on plaques set into the bench); they'd never played in the tournament and had never wanted to, but they'd been playing golf here since long before the tournament had started and so felt as if they owned the bench.

"How's your hand?" Earnie said. They always started this way, testing each other's injuries before they played.

"Old man," said Sandov. Earnie was the older of the two, but he was always Earnie, his first name, while Sandov was always Sandov, his last name.

The wall clock said eleven thirty, their usual starting time. The four ladies were well off the tee now, but the young man Earnie had seen earlier was carting a bag—a huge bag with at least fifteen clubs and with red woolen socks covering the five drivers—to the tee. Earnie nudged Sandov, and together they glanced at the starter's booth. They were never paired off, and they wondered why they were being started now with this *stranger,* but Steve, the old starter, wasn't there. The new starter, Richard, the "teenager," as they called him, had taken his place.

The young man left his bag by the box and headed to the drinking fountain, and Sandov walked over to look at the clubs. Manufactured by a company he had never heard of, the clubs had shafts made out of that graphite stuff; the backsides of the irons, shiny with new brass, had three strange holes about a quarter of an inch wide and lined up from the heel to the toe. The hole in the toe of each club had a small weight inserted into it. To improve balance, Sandov thought with contempt. He walked back over to Earnie and shrugged.

"Young tourists," said Sandov. "Always have to have a new set of clubs when they come to Vegas."

"At least it's not summer," Earnie said, and Sandov smiled. Last summer, two tourists from California—why did the dumbest tourists come from there?—had teed off at noon on the hottest day of the year, not taking any liquids with them, not wearing hats, not bothering with a cart because they wanted to save money. They'd both had heart attacks on the fourteenth fairway. The ambulance had torn up tire marks on five fairways getting to the men.

He and Sandov lifted their bags from the stand by the shop door. They each had only seven clubs, the only clubs they'd ever needed: driver, three-, five-, seven-, and nine-irons, a sand wedge, and a putter. They'd picked up the clubs here and there before the sixties had come and they'd decided that clubs couldn't get any better. The top layers of chrome and nickel had worn from Sandov's old Spalding putter, the oldest club either of them had, and the bright brass beneath, polished smooth by years of contact with manicured greens, flashed in the sunlight as they carried their bags to the tee.

The young man returned and stepped onto the tee ahead of them, and he swung through several practice drives with the regularity of a pendulum. His biceps and forearms bulged from his green Greg Norman shirt, and gray woolen slacks wrapped around his torso and thighs, revealing well-formed muscles with each of his swings. When he finished, he wiped his mustache and pulled a tee from his bag to clean the mud from his spikes. The black-and-white leather uppers made his spikes look more like spats, get-up shoes, than golf shoes.

"You up, dandy?" said Earnie.

The man smiled at them and stepped up to his ball. With a whir and a crack, the ball flashed away from them, then seemed to slow down as a ball does when it goes out a distance from the tee. The ball rose toward the peak of Mount Charleston, sensing the sky beyond, then it leveled out, then it sank, then it landed and bounced twice on the green, two hundred and eighty yards away.

Earnie and Sandov stared. The dandy was a big hitter, but his drive had been pure and straight, and he had cleared the inlet from the lake, which split the fairway at two hundred and fifty yards, and which most big hitters fell into when they tried to drive the green. It was unheard of—it was treasonous. Earnie and Sandov both hit their balls well short of the water, then used their seven-irons to chip onto the green, all the time feeling the smile of the younger man warming their backs.

All of them two-putted, but for Earnie and Sandov that meant pars, while the young man had birdied.

"What's your name?" Earnie asked him.

"John Stallings. You?"

"Earnie Davidson. Just call me Earnie."

Sandov winced.

"You ever had lessons?" Earnie asked John.

"Dad was the leader of the Navy team down in San Diego during the Korean War."

"You're in your thirties, then?"

John nodded.

Earnie glanced at Sandov as if expecting him to join in and help sound out the stranger, but Sandov polished the head of his three-iron as John stepped to the second tee and drove.

Another long, straight shot, avoiding the trees to the left and the houses to the right. The ball sailed over the sand traps guarding the front left and front right sides of the green and landed five feet from the pin.

"Five-iron, huh?" said Earnie, pulling out his three-iron. He and Sandov both got on the green as well, but John one-putted for another birdie, while Earnie and Sandov two-putted for par.

"Where d'you play usually?" Earnie asked John.

"I'm still in San Diego," he said. "Torrey Pines."

"Yeah, sure, we've played there," said Earnie.

Sandov watched John tee up on the third hole, a dog-eared left that wandered along the lake for three hundred and fifty yards. John seemed like a nice sort, but Earnie was being too friendly, and Sandov felt like his old friend was giving away family secrets every time he talked with the other man.

John didn't quite drive to the green this time, and all three of them settled the hole with pars. They'd caught up with the four ladies who'd started ahead of them, and they waited on the cart path behind the tee box as the ladies finished their drives.

"Nice set of clubs," Earnie said to John.

"They're not on the market yet." John pulled out his three-iron and showed Earnie how the weight screwed into the holes on the club head. He also brought out a bag of extra weights, some made of brass, some of iron, and some of aluminum. Each metal had a different weight, and with them he could adjust the club head to the balance best for him. Earnie, despite his initial distrust of the new-fangled clubs, felt himself growing interested.

"Now that old putter," John said, pointing at Sandov's bag, "That's a neat old club. My dad had one like it."

Earnie and John both looked at Sandov; Sandov stared at Earnie. "It's just an old putter," Sandov said.

"We had quite a time finding it," said Earnie, and he told John the story of how after World War II, just after he and Sandov had met, they had driven all the way to Los Angeles on old Route 66 to find good putters. "We didn't look for the latest models. We looked for the clubs with the best feel, you know what I mean, the magic. We wanted clubs that would sink the tough putts. Boy, did we look. Problem was, all the clubs made around wartime skimped on metals to help the war effort. But we finally found a shop in Pasadena—"

"Arcadia," said Sandov.

"Arcadia," said Earnie—he remembered it being Pasadena. "Anyways, the shop had some used clubs from the thirties—the old kind, solid, heavy clubs with hickory shafts and leather grips. The prices were so good that after we bought the putters, we bought starter sets, too, even though the rest of the set didn't have the same feel to them. But we found other clubs, one by one, over the years, that had the magic of those first putters, and we replaced the older clubs only when we were sure that the newer clubs felt better."

Sandov took the putter from the bag and polished the head over and over while Earnie spoke, taking deep breaths, turning his back to them as if studying the fairway ahead. He waited for Earnie to stop the story before the final episode. Sandov remembered the rest: that the last club Earnie had replaced was, ironically, his putter. Earnie and Sandov had fought over that one and had almost split apart, but Sandov had eventually grown used to the club, and Earnie had promised that he wouldn't buy another club without his friend's approval. But that had been their last purchase. The clubs since the sixties had not been made with the same magic, and that was why, Sandov smiled wryly, these young pros they saw on TV nowadays couldn't shoot any better than the older pros like Hogan and Snead. Earnie and Sandov both liked Ben Crenshaw, for he alone among the young guys stuck with his old putter.

Earnie was taking a few swings with John's club, though it was too long for him.

"Choke up on it," John said.

Earnie did, and he liked the club so much even choking up that he used it on his drive.

Sandov heard the *ping!* and thought the ball sounded like a squashed tin can when it hit the club. But Earnie's shot had the same beautiful arc that John's shots had had, and the ball dropped dead on the green.

Sandov refused John's offer to try one of the clubs, but he couldn't clear his thoughts and focus on the concentrating blank that helped calm his nerves when he shot. He tried to put too much on the ball, and his drive fluttered into the lake.

"You okay?" Earnie asked him. Sandov shrugged and jammed his club back into his bag.

After that hole, Earnie stuck with his old clubs. He had fallen under the Tom Kite Syndrome, a disease he and Sandov had named after reading a *Sports Illustrated* article that showed the pro golfer's workshop and detailed the amount of time he spent fiddling with his clubs and changing the angles of their faces for that extra edge, that so-called "control." When they'd read about Kite's enthusiasm for the "2½ iron" he'd created, they'd put the magazine down in disgust.

But John didn't obsess over his equipment. John, on vacation, was testing the clubs for a friend here in town who worked for the company, but he wasn't taking any money to do so. He was simply interested in the new clubs. And from the conversations they had as they wound through the rest of the course, Earnie picked up in John's words a true sportsman's love for golf, a true desire to play for the playing's sake—against the course and against himself and not against other people or "the damn clubs he'd bought," as other golfers would complain. John had turned down a scholarship to play back East so he could go to school in San Diego and help his father in their family's carpeting business, and he and his father never

played in any of the local tournaments down their way—not even
when the Navy called up John's dad and asked him to play for old
times' sake.

At the end of eighteen holes, John led Earnie by five strokes, and
Sandov had drifted to six behind Earnie, a bad day for him. There
they parted—John had paid for another round, and Earnie and Sandov went into the bar for their afternoon drinks. They sat across
from each other on the patio at the wrought-iron table under the
hanging geranium and watched John march over the bridge to the
first green—on in one stroke again.

"He's good," Earnie said.

"Too young," said Sandov.

Earnie fingered the card John had given him. On it was the
phone number and the address of the friend who'd given John his
clubs. Sandov eyed it as he finished his vodka.

"Those clubs have the right feel to them," Earnie said.

"They're machines," said Sandov. He pointed to the Champions'
Bench. "*That* has the right feeling."

Earnie put the card back into his pocket.

Naked City

JOSÉ SKINNER

The phone rang Sunday morning, just as Ernie was waking. His wife, Dorothy—Dot—was already up: he heard her padding around the living room. He suspected she was nude, and this excited him. It was midsummer, and they both, now that their last daughter, Lisa, had finally left the nest, often went nude around the house. Yesterday morning Ernie asked Dot if she wouldn't mind wearing just her apron so he could watch her naked rump, white as the enamel of the stove, while she cooked their breakfast eggs, a suggestion that she pretended scandalized her.

Dot answered the phone. That she was speaking on the phone nude excited Ernie further, and that it was apparently a stranger on the other end, even more. It had been months, possibly years, since he had been so aroused in the morning—it took him way back, to drowsy Sundays in church, when he sat on the acolyte's plush chair, listening to the congregation's mumbled prayers, his own prayer to God being that his uncontrollable boner might go down and his satin robes might not tent out in front of him when the time came for him to approach the altar and snuff the candles. In more recent years, had he still been a praying man, he might have prayed to *get* an erection—at one point last fall, he had concluded that his potency was as thoroughly extinguished as those candles. Which made the present excitement, achieved without the help of any little blue pill, all the more miraculous.

She murmured into the phone with guarded consent. Then she said, "How big? How many inches?"

Ernie rose up in bed on his elbows. This was a very interesting conversation his wife was having.

"All color? Uh-huh. Three couples and three single poses." Her voice was husky. With sleep, or with arousal? "Air-brushed, what's that? Oh. Well, but I want them to be realistic. Not warts and all, but—" She giggled. "Okay. All right, that'll be fine."

This was incredible. He'd read, in one of the many magazines he subscribed to since retiring, that women purchased 40 percent of the pornography these days; but it was unbelievable that his sixty-year-old wife, while not an entirely conservative person, would agree to buy smut from a telephone salesman. And peddling pornography by telephone, that had to be illegal, even in Las Vegas!

She was buying it for both of them, no doubt—the same article said women bought porn not so much for themselves, but to share with their husbands or boyfriends. He snuggled into the sheets and squeezed his miracle. He and Dot were having a sexual renaissance for sure.

"Ernie? Are you up yet?" she called.

"Junior's up," he called back. "Let's dunk his head."

Dot went in the bedroom. "Put him away," she said. She stepped into panties. "A man just called from a photo studio. They've got a special today. Now's our chance to get those portraits Lisa's been nagging at us for, without having to spend a fortune."

Almost as incredible as the idea of a telephone smut salesman was the idea that someone would cold-call trying to sell studio portraits. On a Sunday morning, to boot. As if people were just sitting around thinking how much they needed their pictures taken! But obviously it had worked with Dot.

"When?" he asked petulantly. He was a little annoyed that Dot had scarcely noticed the miracle of his stiffy. And he hated getting his picture taken.

"Today at three, at Food Frontier. They've set up a little studio in the back. I'm going out now to get some of the big curlers. You be thinking about what you want to wear. Something on the dark side looks best, the man said."

A portrait for daughter Lisa. Ever since Lisa had landed a job and a cubicle at Signal Communications and Aerospace Technology—SCAT, as its laid-off former employees, including Ernie, called it—she'd wanted a picture of them to put on her desk. He should be flattered: most office people had pictures of their mates and children, and if they didn't have a mate or children, as Lisa didn't, they put out pictures of their cat or dog. But rarely of their parents.

Lisa had never had a good job before this one. As soon as she had turned eighteen she had taken off for Hollywood, waitressing and whatnot while trying to break into the movie business. After a couple of years of that, she came back home, haggard and defeated. She lived with her parents while studying computers at Vo-Tec, then three months ago she landed the job at Signal and moved into her own place.

Ernie had worked at SCAT's assembly plant in Henderson for twenty years before getting laid off at the same time Lisa was hired. He liked to think she'd gotten the job, at least in part, on the strength of his rock-steady record at the company. What he didn't like was that she worked precisely for the department most responsible for forcing him into early retirement: Cybernetics and Terotechnology, which developed robots to displace people like him. The company called the layoffs and forced retirements "downsizing" and "telescoping."

Ernie looked down at his erection. "Downsize, junior, we gotta go. Telescope yourself, you one-eyed bandit!"

The telephone rang again. Ernie tugged on his shorts before answering. Unlike Dot, he could never answer the telephone naked. Who was to say every modern telephone didn't have some kind of tiny video camera embedded in it that allowed certain callers with access to the right equipment to see the person answering? Dot thought this ridiculous, but he reminded her of all the sophisticated surveillance equipment manufactured at places like SCAT. "Lie naked on the back patio," he had warned her just the day before, "and a satellite'll count every hair on your ass!" "I don't have hair on my ass," she replied. "That's what I mean," said Ernie.

"Hi, Dad? It's Lisa."

"Speak of the devil," said Ernie. He told her about the photography session. Did she want two photographs of them singly, one as a couple, or what?

"How about at least two of you together, plus some singles? I need a set at work and one at home. And get them big enough so I can *see* you guys, Dad, not little passport pictures."

Again, he knew he should be flattered, but he felt like saying: You going to pay for them, little girl? Her present salary was larger than his early retirement income, that was for sure. Well, he should be happy for her, happy that she had a desk to put pictures on. The guys on the factory floor had to carry their tattered family pictures around in their wallets.

"How're the robots coming along?" he asked.

"Oh, Dad, I don't want talk about work now. It's Sunday."

"Twenty years," he said, "and I called in sick only four times."

"But a robot doesn't even *sneeze,* Dad. Oh, here you've got me talking about them again like they're these little silver men."

A robot doesn't sneeze. Or have dirty thoughts. He remembered the day on the assembly line when he found himself gazing up at the boost straps above the line, fantasizing dangling naked from them with all the women in the plant blowing on his parts with air hoses as he bobbed along. Distracted by this fantasy, he forgot to pull the fuse wires, and the whole line had to be shut down for the morning.

"So why do people," Ernie asked his wife when she got back, "display pictures of their loved ones at work?"

"Why do you think? It's to remind them of the people they care about, and who care about them."

He wanted to say: She's run me out of a job, how is that caring?

"It's like protection," Dot added.

Dot looked good in her black skirt and silver concho belt and solid purple blouse. Ernie decided to wear his navy blue blazer and paisley silk ascot to the photo session. An ascot was particularly ridiculous on a summer afternoon, but he'd never worn it before, and now seemed the time to. Lisa had given it to him when she was a teenager, for Father's Day. It was billowy and feminine and soft, yet manly. It gave him a funny feeling of strength and vulnerability, like he used to get when he put on his acolyte's robe, half a century ago; or even before that, when he was five or six years old and would pose in front of the mirror, naked except for his tiny red cowboy boots and a bright silver gun in a holster.

Ernie set the house alarm, beeped off the car alarm, and he and Dot climbed into the hell-hot Chrysler and eased down the driveway. They lived in Meadows Village, near the top of the Strip. It had once been an excellent neighborhood, nicknamed Naked City because of all the showgirls who lived there. Those girls had a propensity for nude sunbathing. You went into an apartment complex and there they'd be, lying naked around the pool. They had to be tan for their jobs. It was hard not to stare.

But then the Marielito Cubans and other riffraff had moved in, and the showgirls left. Now it was bustling with crime and drugs. The brand-new Stratosphere Tower was supposed to "shine like a beacon of progress" over the neighborhood and cleanse it, but this hadn't happened yet. It almost made you want to move, if you could afford it, to a place like Summerlin, that Howard Hughes Corp. master-planned community being built on the west side, which was going to make the original planned community, Boulder City, look positively chaotic by comparison. They said fiber optics were going to be laid to every curb so that each home could be wired with the most sophisticated security and computer systems. "Future-proofing," the Hughes people called it. Lisa said she was saving for a Summerlin home.

The improvised photo studio was set up, as Dot had told him, in the back of the Food Frontier supermarket, but somehow he didn't think that meant the actual storage and processing area. It was an incongruous place for getting your portrait taken; it was like when they'd celebrate some guy's birthday on the factory floor, bright pink cake and a balloon or two in the midst of all that gray grease and machinery.

They were directed through stacks of lettuce boxes and bitter-smelling cauliflower, past the break room where smocked employees sat smoking in silence, and up a flight of metal stairs to another dim room, where a small man in a tropical shirt greeted them. This was Rudy Diamond, the photographer. He had thin, hairy arms and a craggy smile, and rings on every finger.

Rudy Diamond lit a corner of the room with a powerful lamp and had Dot sit on a childishly small red velvet stool in front of a mottled blue-and-green screen. He brushed a wisp of hair from her cheek, backed up, ducked under the shroud of his old-fashioned camera and took some shots. Ernie grew warm under his ascot. He could hear whacking sounds from below, and smelled fresh meat.

Ernie was next. Rudy smoothed Ernie's unruly eyebrows with gentle strokes of his long, ringed fingers, and then placed his hands on either side of Ernie's head, like the priest used to do, and for a moment Ernie, hypnotized, imagined him kissing his forehead in blessing. Rudy tilted Ernie's head to the side, told him to hold it right there, and ducked to his camera.

After the solo shots were done, Rudy produced a peculiar sort of double seat, also upholstered in red velvet, from behind the screen. He had them sit on it together, Ernie behind Dot.

"Scoot back just a little," Rudy told Dot, and she did, until her rump wedged firm in Ernie's crotch. He placed Ernie's arm gently across Dot's chest so that his forearm nestled beneath her left breast.

"That's right, just a *little* more lovey-dovey," said Rudy from beneath his shroud.

Dot settled back softly against Ernie, and he snuggled up to her. He got hard. He hoped she could feel it through his knit slacks.

"Just a *couple* more exposures," Rudy said.

Suddenly it occurred to Ernie: Rudy Diamond does porn. He's a porn guy. Twin drops of cold sweat rolled down either side of his spine as he imagined Rudy taking him aside, telling him in low tones that if he and the Mrs. wished some exposures of intimate poses, something for a private collection, then that could certainly be arranged. . . .

"One week from today," Rudy announced. "Pick them up right here."

Ernie took the receipt with a quaking hand.

"I'm glad that's over," Dot said as they walked out of the supermarket. "That Rudy Diamond, what a sleaze."

"Sleaze?" Ernie said.

"Sleaze."

Back home, Dot changed into her gardening clothes and went outside to tend her tomatoes, defying the heat. He imagined her naked except for the orange sweatband and tennis shoes, bending over her beds. And why not? Their backyard was private, at least that corner of it. And this was Naked City, after all. He might suggest this to her. But at what point would she begin thinking of him as a pervert? Now it worried him that he had gotten excited back there at the photo session.

"Why is Rudy Diamond sleazy?" he asked when she came in for a drink.

"He just reminded me of those modeling agency men Lisa said crawl all over Hollywood. Preying on kids like her."

Ernie remembered Lisa alluding, in dark tones, to those agencies. She hadn't gone into detail about them—at least not with him—but now it occurred to him, with a stab, that maybe they had tried to force her into pornography.

"Did she . . ." he began to ask. "Never mind."

Ernie got an erection the next morning in bed, but it collapsed like the imploded Dunes tower when he became fully conscious and remembered what Dot had said about Lisa being preyed upon in Hollywood. It bothered him to think he had never worried much about her, much less gone out to see how she was doing. He liked to say a Vegas-raised girl knows how to take care of herself, though he knew better than anybody that this was a myth, that not everybody in Las Vegas was streetwise. He himself knew next to nothing about the Mob, gambling, showbiz, all those Vegas things. He was a working stiff. And the fact was, he had been too damned tired to travel to see her, what with the mandatory overtime at the plant and all. The plant had used him up there at the end before tossing him out.

No, he wasn't used up: Junior was back, after all. Though Ernie couldn't quite remember what they involved, the fantasies that brought Junior to life again this morning were no doubt pornographic. What fantasies weren't? Still, he was no smut hound. He found strip shows ridiculous, not to mention expensive. He had seen exactly two adult movies in his life, and he hadn't particularly liked either one. In theory, it was exciting to see people have at it, but these were actors, and so bad they didn't know how to act as though they weren't acting. They looked right into the camera for instruction. They were too obviously *working,* and that turned him off. Robots made of flesh. Prostitutes turned him off for the same reason. Working girls. Those showgirls sunning their naked bodies around the pool: working on their tans. Work, work, work, that's all anybody did.

Lisa worked like a dog at SCAT, running the computers that ran the robots. The surveillance was the killer, according to her. The girls in data processing had their every keystroke monitored, their performance evaluated by how many strokes they did per hour. The company tried to make it sound like a positive thing by giving bonuses to those operators who made quota. Lisa called the bonuses slot money because most of the girls spent them feeding slot machines. Ernie imagined a scheme whereby the girls' earnings, as measured by keystroke, could be channeled directly to those slot machines, so they could play while working. How about that for automation? In the old days, they put a pail of feed around a horse's neck to keep him going round and round the mill, which was pretty much the same thing.

Ernie called Lisa to tell her he and her mother had gotten their pictures taken, and they'd be ready Sunday. She could come over and get them then, or they could drop them off.

"Except I'll be at work Sunday, is the thing."

"Working Sundays? Last Sunday, as I remember, you didn't even want to *talk* about work."

"I didn't exactly choose to go in. But our team's running a new program and it takes awhile."

"So come over after work."

"I don't know when that'll be, Dad. It could be late."

"Well. Whenever. We'll be here."

Sunday came fast, and it caught Ernie uneasy. Eyes were everywhere. In the old days, the only public surveillance you had to worry about, and then only if you were a cheater, were those eyes in the skies at the casinos. Now, as he and Dot drove to Food Frontier, he glanced up at the stoplights to see if he could make out the cameras the police department was said to have ordered from SCAT, the ones that snapped a picture of every license plate and sent an automatic ticket to all speeders and red-light runners. Inside Food Frontier, as he waited for his cash to be pumped from the ATM, he stared into the camera lens barely visible behind the opaque glass and recalled reading somewhere that these cameras took a picture of your iris, whose flecks and striations were as unique as fingerprints. And he remembered some guys at the plant talking about a chip being developed that could be implanted into the human optic nerve and record everything a person saw.

"Remind me to get milk when we come out," Dot said, and Ernie imagined sticking his hand into the dairy cooler, where an X-ray–type device would immediately read his cholesterol level, displaying it in red digital numbers on the cooler's aluminum facing.

Rudy Diamond had their pictures spread out on a card table in the studio. Their broad faces stood brightly pale against the blue background and the darkness of their clothing. The size of the three portraits of him and Dot together on the double seat shocked him: each was as big as a magazine page. In two of those pictures they wore dreamy expressions; but in the third, Ernie's was somewhere between excited and frightened, his nostrils slightly flared, his mouth falling from smile to embarrassment. That must have been the moment when it occurred to him that Rudy was maybe a porn guy. Now Ernie imagined himself and Dot with their clothes off on that odd loveseat, Dot leaning back, her ample white ass-cheeks hugging the lush velvet, Ernie pressing into her, about to—

"Mix and match," said Rudy. "Take only the ones you like."

Ernie kept staring at the pictures. He was afraid if he looked at Rudy, Rudy would read his mind. Fortunately, Dot did the talking.

"We'll take two of these big ones," she said, all business with the sleaze Rudy Diamond. "These two; he looks funny in this other one. And we'll take the singles. I guess we can take one of each of the singles, so she can choose, don't you think, Ernie?"

Ernie nodded. He was thinking about what it would be like to be an unwitting father opening a dirty magazine to find his buck-naked daughter gazing salaciously at him. Holy smokes.

Ernie couldn't wait to get out of there. He let Dot get the milk, but when she mentioned looking for frames for the pictures, he said, "Lisa can get the frames she wants. Come on, let's go."

When they got home, Ernie suggested she put the milk away and they go right now to the SCAT offices and deliver the pictures to Lisa.

"What's the rush?" said Dot. "She'll come get them when she can."

"Who knows when she can? She works all the time. She wants the pictures, we've got the pictures. I'm saying, let's just get it done and over with."

"It's too hot to drive out there now. Besides, I don't feel right going to the workplace. Do you ever remember me going to see you at the plant?"

"Well, I'm going. I'm her father. And I worked there twenty years. I guess I have a right."

The SCAT office complex was located on Howard Hughes Parkway. It made sense that the headquarters of a company devoted to the manufacture of surveillance equipment would be on a street named for a famously paranoid guy. Dot was right; it was hot, the midday photons pouring down from the upended sun. But the sweat would have trickled down his spine even if it had been cold, because the buildings made him nervous, all opaque glass, a thousand eyes in reflective sunglasses. In his twenty years with SCAT, he had never entered these offices.

But he wasn't about to chicken out now. He strode boldly up the marble steps and pulled open the heavy glass door. The guard in the foyer stopped him, had him state his business. The guard made a phone call and they waited in the cool silence.

Lisa's heels clopped smartly down the hall. "Wow, Dad, you didn't have to deliver these," she said, taking the envelope of pictures and casting the guard a my-funny-old-dad look.

"I didn't have to, but I wanted to," he said, offended by her complicity with the guard. She had plenty to learn about pecking orders if she thought she had to buddy up to a weekend security cop.

Then, to his mortification, she took the pictures out right there and showed them to the guard, who nodded.

"You two lovebirds," she said as she gazed upon the ones of him and Dot together. Ernie flushed.

"Come on up, Dad," Lisa said. "I'll show you what we're working on."

The floor she took him to was a sea of cubicles. Heads popped up like prairie dogs to see who the man with the unfamiliar voice was. He expected her to show him one of the famous robots, but her cubicle was only full of computer stuff and books and printouts.

"Where do you think you'll put the pictures?" Ernie asked. "We didn't get frames. We thought you'd get your own frames."

"Don't worry about it. For now I'll tack them to the wall. Very carefully, no holes."

There were a few other things tacked to the corkboard wall: a couple of yellowed Dilbert cartoons from the newspaper, a map showing how to get out of the maze of cubicles, and a photocopied cartoon of a fish swimming in an unplugged blender. "I can't stand the stress," the fish said.

"You get a lot of stress on this job?" Ernie asked his daughter quietly.

"Oh, that's just a joke. Everybody has cartoons in their areas." Then, loud enough so that others could hear: "I like my job, Dad."

A stooped man with a skinny neck and bobbing Adam's apple came into Lisa's cubicle with some more printouts. Lisa introduced him as Jeff, but the name on his ID badge said Geoff. Ernie believed he saw pity wound Geoff's bespectacled eyes as he gazed upon the downsized father, the old guy replaced by their robots.

Geoff and Lisa stood very close to one another as they looked over the printouts. Ernie thought their hands were possibly touching. Maybe they'd get married. In the wedding chapel at the top of the Stratosphere, say. What did they call guys like that? Nerds, or was it geeks? Harmless, anyway, which was as much as you could hope for in this world of Rudy Diamonds.

"Dad, I've got to go help Geoff for a minute. Oh, let me put you on the Internet. I've always been wanting to show you the Net. We've just got to get you and Mom a computer." She fiddled around with the mouse and told him all he had to do was type in something.

"The search engine's on Excite," she said, whatever that meant. "Type in anything, the first thing that comes to mind. Then point and click to surf it." Whatever *that* meant. "I'll be back in a few."

Ernie settled into the swivel chair. Yes, that's what it said, Excite, the letters actually exploding with excitement. First thing that comes to mind, I don't know,

Naked. He typed in "Naked."

He should have known. The Internet was said to be full of pornography, and sure enough, here came something called Live Sexstream, a banner of naked people flowing across the screen, flanked by winking pictures of legs crossing and uncrossing.

This is wrong, he said to himself. Point and click. He did what he'd seen Lisa do, and then one of the winking pictures in the corner began to unfold slowly on the screen, pixel by pixel, hugely, a naked woman with her legs parted right in his face.

He heard his daughter's voice down the hall. "Oh, Geoff, I forgot the floppy. Let me go back and get it." Point and click, point and click, get it off.

Point and click, no good. Type something. No effect. The woman kept unfurling before him, inexorable. His daughter's thumping footsteps, growing closer. The screen blinked to a moment of blankness, then the naked woman burst back on, in even greater detail. Ernie jumped out of his seat and pulled the plug.

"Dad, what are you doing?" Lisa shrieked. "We're running an application, you can't—"

She jammed the plug back into the surge trap and plunged herself in her chair and started typing furiously. Ernie glanced around the vast room. The prairie dogs, who'd popped up at the sound of her distress, fell back into their holes like targets in a carnival game.

"I'm sorry," Ernie said. "It was doing something strange, so—"

"I think it'll be okay."

"I hope so, I really do. Well. I guess I better go."

"Okay, thanks, Dad, thanks for the pictures." She didn't look up. "I'll call you guys."

Ernie snaked his way out of the cubicle maze and headed for home, leaving behind him the shimmering office buildings. Lisa was going to be all right. She knew computers, and she was working overtime. SCAT had a contract to launch satellites from the Test Site, so it looked like things might be steady for the company for a while. Maybe she would get her future-proofed house in Summerlin sooner than she thought. He hoped he hadn't screwed her up when he unplugged the computer, he really did.

And if the company got rid of her the way it had gotten rid of him, she could just come back home. Naked City wasn't as bad as its reputation. True, it had a lot of places like this Gecko's All Nude Showclub he was driving past right now. Gecko's, gawko's. In the dimness inside, lizards along the wall, gaping. In the brightness outside, a woman in a bubblegum-pink skirt, watching him without seeming to watch.

But even closer to home stood a white stucco church—a real church, not a Vegas wedding chapel. As he drove past, he saw its lot ablaze with cars: some kind of late mass. No, a wedding, or a renewal of vows: in front of its dazzling whiteness stood an elderly black couple, the woman in a white dress and the man in a white suit, his hair white too. When Ernie blinked he saw an afterimage of a young white couple in dark dress.

Dot, still damp from the shower, stood naked in front of the fan—trying, as usual, to save a few bucks by not running the AC.

"How's our daughter?" she asked.

"She's got some stress. But she can handle it. I hope."

"Well, she's got her protection now."

Dot squatted a little to let the fan blow between her legs. Water jeweled there. She smiled at Ernie. Ernie shut the blinds.

During their lovemaking, he glanced in the bureau mirror and saw the strength in Dot's arched back and the vigor in his thrusting haunches. He thought of the velvet double loveseat and the positions they might still be able to manage on such a contraption, and it brought him to climax. Afterward, lying sweatily next to Dot, it occurred to him that Lisa might at that very moment be pinning their picture up, gazing at them fondly, and it gave him the funny feeling again, the feeling he had gotten as a child naked in his boots, or as an acolyte in his robes. He wondered where that feeling came from, what it meant, or whether it was important to know these things. All he knew right now for sure was that he had the rest of his life, all the time in the world, to figure it out.

Big-City Detective

JOHN L. SMITH

Around the Silver Lake Café and the greater Baker area they called me Lucky Jack Brown, but I wasn't feeling all that fortunate. Overall, I was the same Jack I'd always been, if you didn't count the fact my right leg ended at the knee and buying work boots was no longer a priority. Throw in the eye I was missing, and I was beginning to look like a pirate, or a Mr. Potato Head with parts lost.

I was working on my second cup of coffee at the café when it occurred to me that what doesn't kill you doesn't always make you stronger, but can leave you with a monthly disability check and your mornings free. Three quarters of me was living proof.

I had taken to wearing a fake leg, the one they issued me at the hospital a dozen weeks after the accident at the plant. With practice, they told me, I'd be back on my feet in no time. Back on my foot is more like it. It's a little like dancing drunk on roller skates until you get the hang of it. Once the skin around the stump toughened up, I was back in business. Just forget about trying out for the Dodgers. If I concentrate I can walk uphill without looking like a wine rummy, but my one-eyed big-league dreams are dashed for good.

A guy wants to do a lot of things as a kid, but he seldom gets to do any of them. Until my leg problem, I made a living with a shovel. A lot of nights when I was younger I'd lay back and think about being a ballplayer with the class of Koufax, the power of Frank Howard, and the toughness of Johnny Roseboro. But it's a long way from Baker to the big leagues.

When I was real little I wanted to be a swashbuckling buccaneer or Buck Rogers's best buddy and fly all over the universe and rub elbows with aliens from other worlds and disintegrate them with a radar gun, and maybe I'd save old Buck's hide once in a while just to prove myself worthy and maybe get promoted to Double Star General or Commander of all the spaceships. It was just a kid's game, though. The only guy who ever saw a spaceship in the sky above Baker was Crazy Tommy the Half-Breed, and that was only after he drank some of Big Frank's antifreeze.

Until I was in the service I never even flew on an airplane, and then it was only once during boot camp before they sent me home after I got my eye knocked out on the obstacle course. The sergeant said I was a one-in-a-million moron, or just real lucky, but I didn't feel so special. I wore an eye patch, which I thought looked pretty stupid. You try explaining how you lost your eye trying to run across a fallen log. It doesn't win you much sympathy from certain girls you know, and no one at the VFW will buy you a beer and call you soldier, but at least it's a true story. The eye pop made it a certainty I'd never go to outer space, not with my weak stomach and lack of depth perception.

Overall, what I wanted most to be was a big-city detective, like in paperback novels and those magazines with the blonds on the covers about to get their throats slit by shadowy figures unknown. But what were the chances I'd find any intrigue spending my life in Baker, California?

Work at National Gypsum had slowed to a trickle even before my right foot slipped off the shovel and got stuck in the rock crusher. I'd been getting three good shifts a week before the accident, a check for $89 a month after they got through with the trimming and slicing. But it wasn't trouble making ends meet because by then Francie and me were all tore up, and the wedding was off and she was getting ready to go off to college in the East studying to be a doctor or a teacher, and so a little money goes a long way when a guy has no girl to impress and take out on dates or dance with, even if I felt like dancing on one leg and a big phony-looking replacement, which looked pretty stupid wearing one of my work boots like I still had a foot to protect. As if no one in town could remember that I was the guy who got his leg tore off. So I took to spending even more time at the Silver Lake Café, where Francie's folks Bea and Big Frank owned the place and ran the gas station out front. They made good money and always got a big kick out of the travelers to and from Las Vegas, and especially their reaction to Barney.

Barney used to peek out from behind the counter and scare rookie truckers halfway to heaven. He had the same effect on old women, too. One time an old woman who was close to blind said to Barney, "Boy, fetch me some more coffee." Apparently she thought Barney was a Negro busboy, although I think he looks somewhat Mexican. I was sitting at the counter having apple pie and coffee when it happened, and I almost choked on my crust, Barney being a chimpanzee and not knowing a word of English or Mexican. It took the woman three times asking, "Boy, boy, can you hear me?" before Barney, who was always dressed in his red suit, hopped up on the counter and stuck his finger in my pie and then jumped down and ran within eyeshot of the old bat. She almost swallowed her upper plate.

And there were all those times we would be sitting at the counter chewing the fat and reading the newspaper from Las Vegas when all of a sudden a scream would echo from the ladies' room toilets. That was Barney again, handing toilet paper to one of the customers.

We all loved Barney. Bea and Frank used to say the chimp had more sense than me and a better chance at marrying Francie, but I knew they were only joking. I had to admit Barney was a beauty and full of personality, and that's why we were all sick as dogs when somebody stole him.

That was in May, and there was all sorts of crying and whining and carrying on by Bea and Francie, and even Big Frank got teary-eyed when he heard the news that somebody'd swiped old Barney.

"Probably that vacuum cleaner salesman from Vegas, the one with the white Ford Coupe and the clean fingernails," Big Frank said one afternoon soon after the incident. "That bastard looked shady and took a liking to Barney from the minute he walked in the café."

"Could have been him," I said, trying to think of maybe some other piece of evidence in time for some quick wit, like the tough operatives in Black Mask. I didn't think of anything. "It seems to me that he's the right guy. You know, maybe."

It never went any further than that for a few weeks, and as the frying-pan-hot summer passed, the crying over Barney stopped, but me and Francie were arguing like two cats over the stupidest things. That's when she sprung college on me like a mousetrap. It about made me sick when I heard the word. Big Frank just looked at me like I was simple when I asked him what the problem with Francie was, and he said no daughter of his was going to marry a desert rat with no real future but a played-out mine. And I said, "Well, how do you like that." I was mad, but I couldn't keep from thinking of her and of all the things we'd talked about over the months. I thought that our friendship and the fact we were from the same town would make a difference, but it didn't. She had her dream of becoming a doctor, and I was just a guy who drank coffee at her folks' café. I felt shipwrecked, or like one of those aliens who is sent to Earth but misses his home planet.

After the middle of August, Francie was getting ready to go away to school and wouldn't have nothing to do with me. So I kept in close proximity to Bea and Big Frank. I was trying to find work that wouldn't get me knocked off disability or make my stump bleed, and on Sundays I'd sit in the corner of the café and drink coffee and listen for any sign or words about when exactly Francie was leaving and about what she was up to. You do strange stuff when you're in love.

I was reading the *Las Vegas Journal* and in the back there was a picture of something that just about made me fall out and shout. On page 17 was a picture of a man and Barney walking down Twain Avenue. It was a picture of the back of the pair, and Barney was still wearing his red busboy outfit. It had to be Barney, and the jerk that was with him could have been the vacuum cleaner salesman. I tore the picture from the newspaper and put it in my pocket.

"What if Barney has been taken to Las Vegas and just can't get back home again?" I asked Big Frank, who didn't like speculation about Barney—especially with Bea making coffee and Francie, Miss Stuck-Up College Gal, within earshot.

"Don't dig that subject up again," he said. "You know that's a sensitive topic in our family."

"Yeah, but what if he was all right and just maybe out loose where someone might find him and return him?"

"Then I'd say that man is a helluva man, real-life Sherlock Holmes—or at least the luckiest sonofabitch to walk the face of God's green Earth."

"You know how much we love Barney," Bea said, wiping the counter and listening to me.

Then Francie came over at the prospect. Well, I thought, Miss

Stuck-Up is sitting up and taking notice. That'd do the trick with her. Then Francie, Big Frank, and Bea would all see I was more than a run-of-the-mill shovel hand. They'd know I was just mild-mannered and underneath was a man they could depend on in any predicament.

Having only been to Las Vegas twice, and both times when I was a kid with bowel trouble that needed a doctor to look into, I wasn't sure where everything was when I got off the bus. I bought a map of the city and sat in the bus station and waited for the sun to rise. I had read where the streets of Sin City were mean, and the folks standing around the bus station at four in the morning weren't exactly Sunday school teachers, so I decided to take care of the business of finding Twain Avenue. I'd brought a change of clothes and a toothbrush with some sandwiches and a coffee thermos in a knapsack. And Nilla wafers for Barney. They're his favorite. I ate the sandwiches before crossing the state line, and the coffee lasted until Jean. I had $74 in my front pocket.

Outside the station, I walked toward the neon lights of Fremont Street. Excitement always makes me hungry, so I walked into the diner at the Golden Gate, took a seat at the counter and ordered a cup of coffee. The place was jumping like Saturday night at the Silver Lake Café, and here it was only Tuesday. I bought another newspaper, hoping to find another clue, but came up empty. I was trying to figure out whether I should buy a piece of apple pie or save my money for cab fare to Twain Avenue, when my concentration was shattered.

"Is this seat taken?" a skinny guy asked, and it was plain to see that it was empty, and in a second my stomach got to hurting and you know what that means: Fag Alert. As I gathered my things, Mr. Friendly said, "Are you sure there's nothing I can help you with? You look lost."

I intended to give him the brush-off, like Bogart, but instead I said, "It's my eye. It wanders when I'm tired. I'm having some trouble focusing on the map."

"New in town?" he asked. "I know my way around pretty well."

"Just got here from Los Angeles," I said. "Looking for Twain Avenue."

"Oh, that's an easy one. I live not far from there. I'll give you a ride."

My good eye must have squinted funny because Mr. Friendly laughed.

"Don't sweat it, sweetheart," he said, extending his hand. "I'm a cabbie. I'm Teddy Riley. Besides, you're not my type."

I was somewhat relieved.

"So what brings you to Las Vegas?" he asked.

I lowered my voice, like the guys I know about do, and said, "I'm here to find a guy."

"You mean like in the movies? Like a detective?" he asked, as light as a kite. His voice sounded like a bird, and I thought everyone in the place would hear him and see us two talking together, and then it didn't matter that I lived in Baker all my life. Somebody'd see me and call me a fairy.

"Hey, keep it down, will ya?"

"Sorry, Lew."

I knew he meant Lew Archer, and it made me feel good to think even that guy'd compare me to him.

"Name's Jack Brown," I said, looking side to side. "How far is it to Twain?"

"It depends on the address."

I pulled out the *Journal* photo from my shirt pocket and unfolded it. Along the sidewalk were tall trees, and I showed Teddy the clipping.

"Maybe the trees will give you an idea of where it is," I said.

"Looks like an area not far from Maryland Parkway, fairly close to the back entrance of the Las Vegas Country Club," Teddy said. "Is this the guy you're looking for?"

I just nodded.

"Do you have a picture of his face?"

I shook my head. "That's it," I said. "That's all I've got to go on. No more clues."

"Well, it really is on my way home," Teddy said. "I'm waiting for my ride. So who's with the man in the photo?" Then he read the cutline. "I was going to say, that's got to be the hairiest boy I've ever seen in my life."

"It's no boy," I said, "It's Barney."

"So that's who you're looking for," Teddy said, waving to a guy in a purple vw Bug as he pulled into the loading zone. "Too bad. I'd be more help finding a man than a monkey."

A vw Bug convertible pulled up outside at the curb. It was Teddy's friend Eddie. Eddie made Teddy look like an ironworker. I nodded my head and got in the back of the vw. With the top down, it was hard to carry on a conversation, which made it easier for me. I didn't have much in common with those guys, although they seemed almost regular sitting there next to each other. Eddie didn't smile at me once or say two words after hello.

During the whole drive the only words I heard him say to Teddy were, "Every stray in southern Nevada."

With Eddie weaving through traffic and racing the engine, it only took us ten minutes to get to an area I thought looked familiar. It was the place in the photograph.

"This is it," Teddy said, after Eddie skidded to a stop at the curb. Teddy handed me a card with the name and phone number of Western Cab Co. "You call if you need some help getting around town," he called as Mr. Personality pulled away and left me at the curb. I put the card in my pocket.

Down the block, I still hadn't seen Barney or the salesman, but I stopped and had four tacos and a large Coke at this little joint with a clerk that only spoke Mexican. It was greasy but good.

I shouldn't have eaten those tacos, because they always give me a sour gut, but a detective's got to keep his strength up. I looked up and down the street for some clues, but couldn't find any. Then I saw St. Francis Veterinary Clinic.

The woman behind the receptionist's desk was immediately familiar to me. She looked a little like you-know-who but was shorter and broader in the beam, with black hair to her shoulders and less makeup. The name tag on her blouse read, "Sarah Ramirez." The second I saw her I would have sworn we grew up together in the Death Valley View Trailer Court on the edge of Baker. She seemed so familiar to me that I couldn't take my eye off her. After a minute I caught myself and looked away before I scared her. One eye staring can be pretty spooky.

"Do you take care of monkeys?" I asked. "You know, chimps and stuff?"

"Yes, sir, we specialize in the treatment of rare and exotic animals and birds. I'm afraid we close early today, but I'll be happy to make an appointment for your animal. But where is your animal?"

"Maybe you can help me," I said, handing her the clipping. "I saw this photo in the newspaper and thought you might be able to help me, whether you know if you've treated that monkey."

She looked at me a little funny, then got the idea.

"You know this man or animal?" she asked.

"You see, I'm looking for a mate," I said, a little embarrassed. "For my monkey, I mean."

She smiled and nodded her head and opened a file cabinet; detective work sure was easy, I thought. All you have to do is be a creative liar.

"Here it is," she said, smiling. Then she said, "Have we known each other before?"

"I was thinking the same thing," I said. "You look so familiar. But I just came to Las Vegas today."

"Let me share with you a little secret," she said softly. "Everyone just got to Las Vegas today."

I thanked her and hit the door. Out on the sidewalk, I could hardly read the notes. The first said, "Charles Gortimer, 1207 Pinehurst, 732-5839." A lot of things were easier when you took the attitude of a big-city detective, I thought.

I spent the rest of the day trying to figure out how to approach this Gortimer fellow, but every time I tried to concentrate the face of Sarah Ramirez interrupted me. I was pretty well lost to the world and once wandered into traffic and almost got hit by a car. I looked in the phone book for her number and found her name and hoped it was the same person. I thought so much about her that I almost forgot about Barney and Baker. By the time I ate lunch and an early dinner, it was too late to call either number.

Don't ever stay the night at the Big Chief Motor Lodge on Fremont Street. Weirdo convention, no kidding. I wound up back downtown in an attempt to save some money on a room for the night. The lock was broken in my room, and all night people were walking back and forth. Women with too much makeup, black guys doing the jive talk and white guys trying to sound like black guys. From the smell of things, my bed had already been slept in. The TV was busted, and the phone didn't work. I cut out the lights and slept in my pants with my prosthesis still attached. They could have my shoes, but that's all they'd get without a fight. It was hell, but the shower worked, and I got an early start in the morning, having breakfast at Winchell's, five cake doughnuts and a bear claw and a couple cups of coffee.

It was a few minutes after six when I started out. It's a good thing, because by the map this Gortimer fellow lived not far from the vet's office. About two miles into the walk, my stump started to blister, and I had to rest.

The house at 1207 Pinehurst was inside the exclusive Las Vegas Country Club. Scaling a wall is next to impossible with my bum leg, so I waited until a moving van pulled up to the security gate and blocked the guard's view. Five minutes later, I was on the sidewalk across the street from Gortimer's fancy brick house, which looked like the kind you usually only see in pictures of Maine. The front lawn was half the size of a football field, and I stood across the street and waited. In a little while, the suspect emerged from the premises without the monkey in question or any other animal. He left in a white Dodge, but I didn't get the license. Since I didn't have wheels of my own, it didn't much matter. I crossed the street. A car passed by, but it didn't see me.

I thought about trying the front door, but I couldn't think of anything clever to make up when someone answered, so I decided to try the side gate and maybe look through a window or two. Bingo. The house backed up to a golf course. Around the back was a cage built right next to the house, a big fancy chicken wire job a dozen feet high with a dead tree and the unmistakable smell of chimp crap all over the floor. But no chimps.

At the back of the cage was a window without glass but a little cloth curtain over it. I leaned close to the screen and tried to see past the curtain, but I couldn't.

"Barney," I said, not trying to be too loud but just enough for the little guy to hear me. "Barney, boy, are you in there?"

Just then a hairy face peeked out from behind the curtain like it was Barney, but without his suit on. Still, his little monkey face was unmistakable. "Barney boy," I said. "It's me, pal. Where's your clothes? Hey, it's me."

Being a real detective was easy, I thought. Then it got tougher. From behind the curtain peeked another face that looked just like Barney, who all of a sudden wasn't paying much attention to me but was sitting in the tree scratching his rump. Barney—well, it could have been Barney—came from out behind the curtain and monkey-shuffled over to the edge of the screen and grinned at me.

"Barney," I said, "you recognize me, don't you, old buddy? Let me get you out of here."

I watched the monkeys pick each other's backs. Monkeys have the right idea. They find a mate, pick her ticks and take good care of her and don't care if she's hairy or not. They find somebody who suits them and stick with her. They don't work at being happy. They're just happy.

I squatted down and took out my pocketknife and began digging in the dirt under the screen. It was murder on the knife, and I'd be embarrassed as hell if someone ever caught me using it for that purpose, but a detective's got to improvise. It took me a few minutes, but I got it done. No one was around when I looked up, only the phony Barney in the tree and the real one sitting picking at monkey doodoo in the dirt. I kept digging, but something caught my eye.

Out from behind the curtain, another monkey appeared. This time, he brought what looked like a twin with him. All four looked like Barney, and I was having trouble spotting the real one.

Especially after another little naked ape hopped out. Then two more, then a little one. The hole was almost dug, and I could put the real Barney on the leash from my knapsack and dress him in one of my work shirts.

"Here, Barney," I said amid the monkey talk. "Come on, pal. It's me."

I took out some of the Nilla wafers I had packed and tossed a couple in the cage near the hole, which was almost big enough for me to fit my head and shoulders under. Here he came, the first Barney from up in the tree. That was the real Barney; my first impressions and instincts were right on. It's always best to trust your first instincts, I always say.

And in a minute, bingo. Barney was sitting in the hole I had dug. The other monkeys were watching and beginning to move closer, sensing that I was one of them and all. I grabbed Barney by the nape of the neck and pulled him under the screen. He bit the holy hell out of my hand, but I was able to slip the leash around his damned neck pretty easily. The blood was all over my pants in no time, but I could tell it wasn't as deep as it felt. I washed it off with a hose and pulled one of my sweat socks over it to help stop the bleeding. Getting a shirt on Barney took about ten minutes; he wasn't happy about getting dressed again, and I guess I don't blame him. It would be nice to hop around with no clothes on and pick ticks and buggers out of your mate's hair, but we had some work left to do.

With Barney in tow, I got the hell out of there as fast as I could. The last I saw them, the chimps were out of their cage and hopping onto the country club's golf course. I shuffled to the corner and called Sarah Ramirez. Barney and I would get along fine as long as the Nilla wafers held out. As I was punching the numbers it dawned on me it was the first time I'd ever called a woman on the phone other than Francie and a few relatives. To my surprise, I wasn't even nervous.

A young girl answered, then called for her mom when I asked for Sarah. She was getting ready for work at the vet center and seemed surprised to be hearing from me. It was a few minutes after seven in the morning.

"Sorry to bother you, but I'm in sort of a jam," I said. "I found my chimp, but I need a ride. I wouldn't normally ask you, but I'm desperate."

She said something in Spanish that sounded like praying, and I asked her what she said.

"I said, 'Give me strength, Saint Francis,'" Sarah Ramirez said.

"Barney's no stray," I replied. "He's a pal, a real friend, but could you bring a bottle of peroxide with you?"

"Peroxide?"

"I'll explain when I see you."

In fifteen minutes, Sarah Ramirez pulled up outside the 7-Eleven in a clean little Chevy Nova. She took one look at my hand and immediately began dressing it with the peroxide and a handful of gauze bandages she had brought with her.

"You don't have to do that," I said, noticing how small and strong her hands were as they held mine.

"This chimp is a friend of yours?"

"Yeah, I guess he's just a little excited."

"You should see a doctor."

"You're close enough for me," I said.

She smiled, "But I am only a receptionist in a veterinary clinic. I have no medical training."

"I'm sure you'll do fine," I said, smiling. "When the bleeding stops, can I take you and your daughter to breakfast?"

She nodded her head in agreement.

"We'll have to leave the monkey behind."

"He's a chimp, actually. Turns out there's a difference."

"Yes, I know."

After we returned Barney to her apartment, and I promised to clean up any of his messes, over breakfast I explained what I had to do, and that Barney wasn't exactly my chimp. She told me about the first time she had seen a monkey. It was in a little traveling circus that came to her hometown, which was Ensenada, Mexico. She quickly said she was a naturalized American with an American daughter to prove it. She had married a serviceman from San Diego. They broke up when she stopped letting him beat her like a rag doll.

"My daughter will not know that life," she said.

"A man would be lucky to have a woman as beautiful as you," I said, my words scaring me as they came out.

She smiled and asked, "Are you sure we haven't met before?"

We talked for more than an hour, but I knew I had unfinished business in Baker.

"You must return the animal to its rightful owner," Sarah said. "That is noble, Jack Brown."

For the first time in my nothing life, I felt noble.

The bus from Las Vegas to Baker was almost empty when I paid for a couple tickets for Barney and me. The driver just shook his head when he took one look at him: "Just make sure he don't crap in my rig." I had him in his little diapers by then, so everything was fine along those lines. He didn't like the drive, but I fed him some fruit, and the time passed without much trouble. Luckily, there were only a few other people on the bus, and they were ugly enough for Barney to be related, so they didn't seem to notice him at all.

I took Barney off the bus and walked him the long way behind the café and looked back to my trailer to hide him for a while until I knew Frank and Bea and Miss Encyclopedia Britannica were together eating dinner. Then they'd be shocked as hell when I came through the door with old Barney boy.

I washed him up and gave him some old clothes of mine, a T-shirt and old knee pants, and to thank me he bit me again, but this time not quite so hard.

Barney seemed happy to be back when I brought him in the front door and let him into the empty dining area. They were eating in the corner.

"Oh, my God," Bea said. "Barney, oh, Barney!"

She was crying before the door closed. Frank was teary-eyed and Francie was whining like a kid.

"Well, I'll be damned, boy. I'll be damned," Big Frank said. "How in the world did you find him?"

I was just about to tell Big Frank all about it when Francie screamed.

"This isn't our Barney," she said. "He's not the same."

"It's just the clothes," I said.

"No, this isn't our ape. He's an impostor."

I was dizzy as hell. My stomach ached and I began to sweat. Tears began to burn my good eye, and I blinked them away. It was then that I learned a life lesson: some people aren't satisfied with anything and don't know how to be grateful. A vision of Sarah Ramirez appeared in my head, and right then I knew what I would do.

I packed up my stuff and locked the trailer. Barney was sitting in a corner of the café fiddling with himself when I opened the door. Bea was in the kitchen and Big Frank was out fixing a guy's flat. Francie was in bed, I guess. Barney came right over to me, and I gathered him up and headed for the Greyhound stop. Bea looked at me, said nothing.

I knew my place was in Las Vegas with all the freaks and strangers, where nobody but Sarah Ramirez knew me. If I was going to get a new start, it would have to be in a new town where a guy could get a second chance without being laughed at.

That's when everything started turning lucky for Jack Brown. There were plenty of jobs I could do, and in a few months I stopped receiving workers' compensation in California. Actually they made me stop and give back $534 in benefits, but I didn't mind. By then Barney and me had moved in with Sarah and Annie, and we're getting married. Sarah says Annie will be the flower girl and Barney the best man. I know she's kidding, of course. Sarah doesn't mind my stump and she likes my two good arms and we laugh about me adopting Annie if she'll adopt Barney. She's the prettiest woman I know.

A few days after moving to Las Vegas, I landed a great job greeting customers at Pirate Bob's Treasure Chest Casino. I wear a wooden leg just like a real shiver-me-timbers buccaneer, and everyone seems to like my uniform. They say it looks very authentic. Little do they know.

You Saw Me Crying in the Chapel

MICHAEL VENTURA

1

She intended to pick a name at random, but when her finger fell upon *Virginia* she laughed—at least, it felt to her like a laugh.

"Random-shamdom."

She wanted to light the book on fire, but she refrained. It was a book of names, one book of many on shelves not far from the checkout register. It listed all possible names, and their lineages, and their meanings. It was a wonderful book, she felt that all of human history was in this book, it was a book that should take the place of the Bible, every root of every name, it *was* a kind of Bible, and so (to Virginia's way of thinking) it really must be burned. But another time.

She took to her new name quickly. Instantly, in fact. It changed her posture, added a bit of stiffness to her spine; it changed the way she held her shoulders, they lifted a little as soon as she read the name; it changed the way her long stringy dirty golden hair felt against her neck—her hair now felt somehow dirtier, somehow heavier, a Virginia should have glistening clean hair; it changed the way her long thin yellow cotton dress felt upon her too skinny body—the dress would caress a Virginia, a virgin, more than it had caressed that other name; it changed the itch in her crotch, that itch of irritation and infection now felt more like something alien was scratching her from without. One of the psychiatrists said her "problem," one of her "problems," was that she had no firm sense of identity; she had said in return—for she always tried to say *something* in return, it was only fair—that the virtue of having very little sense of identity was that one took to new situations rather quickly. "Perhaps too quickly," he'd said. She'd chosen to take that as a joke and laughed politely, or tried to; when the laugh came out, it didn't sound polite.

Oh, she wanted very much to set the book on fire, but she really mustn't. She was seeking something final, and one more arrest was just one more arrest, it wasn't final enough. In any case, as she said aloud, though softly: "It wouldn't do." This was her mother's phrase, and her mother's mother's, and at the moment it meant: it wouldn't do to be arrested in a shop for pregnant women. A shop so pink, a shop so white, a shop shaded with so many pastels. A shop with such generous bras. Such thick shoes that pretended not to be so thick. Such *accessories,* my God! And so many books about baby. Baby, baby, baby. We'll name the baby Virginia.

She was well content with the name. It made that other name, the one that she had answered to—no, rather: the one that she had so persistently failed to answer to—oh, it made that other name seem so common. She was tempted to look up that other unanswerable-to name in the thick paperback name book that she was refraining from burning, but then looking it up seemed a bad idea. For twenty-six years that inappropriate unanswerable-to name had had no meaning for her, and to learn its meaning after she'd discarded it—well, that might weaken her resolve. Not to be what people call "sane," that was one thing; that could be survived, countless people survived *that* every day. But to lose one's resolve— for *that,* the penalties could be severe. She approved of severe penalties as a rule, but not now, not in this ridiculous shop.

Somebody was about to ask her a question. Well, that was inevitable, there were always people doing that. A woman dressed in stern lines. The colors of the woman's fabrics went with the surroundings, light flimsy colors; but the cut of the woman's clothing was stern, as though the colors were pretending to be something else. The woman had a name tag: Gloria. Virginia thanked the fates that her finger had not fallen upon *Gloria;* it was so heavy, she would have had to lie right down on the floor, and she *would* have lain down on the floor right there and never have gotten up if she'd had to carry such a name as Gloria. This stern-cut woman approaching her seemed, to Virginia, as though *she'd* wanted to lie down on the floor all her life, and wanted to right now, but did not have the courage, or the resolve, or the identity, or the lack of identity, or whatever it takes to lie down on the floor if you feel like it.

Gloria seemed to approach in slow motion. She was no older than Virginia, and not much larger, but she looked as though she was trying to pretend that she was both. Virginia resented this mightily. There was no reason for it. People should have to pay for taking such liberties.

"Can I help you?" the Gloria person asked.

"What did you have in mind?" Virginia asked back. She felt a little guilty. She'd stolen the retort from a movie, and it was her firm, even fanatical, belief that we pay for anything we steal in any way from the movies. But there, it was said, no taking it back. She wasn't good at taking things back anyway.

"Look, is there something you'd like to buy? Would you like a suggestion?"

"I'd love one. *Please* suggest something to me, *Gloria.* I think you'd better do that, suggest something to me right now."

"I think you'd better leave, ma'am."

"But I'm pregnant. Where else can I go?"

The Gloria-person's face dissolved a little. There was somebody underneath it, peeking out, somebody who wasn't called Gloria at all, somebody who shouldn't have to pay anymore for anything, someone who'd paid too much as it is. And *that* person said:

"Please find somewhere else to do this."

Virginia smiled. *Really* smiled, for the first time in a while. There was something golden, something shining, in Virginia's smile, no matter how many times that smile had been misinterpreted (especially by men, though Virginia had found that women were no slouches at misinterpretation). And so Virginia felt herself smile with that golden lost thing in her. She smiled at whoever wasn't Gloria in the Gloria-person.

"Hey in there," she said, smiling. "Hey. Hi. Ask and it shall be given. See? I'm history."

And she swirled around, Virginia did, and walked elegantly, like the princess she'd once imagined herself to be, walked from the coolness of that ridiculous shop out into the brutal Las Vegas sun, bestowing the favor of her absence upon both the person who the Gloria was afraid to be and that person-within who was afraid to be

Gloria. Virginia was so happy to see *that* person, that not-Gloria, that she would have given *her* anything, but all that had been asked was absence. Well, she could do that, she was good at bestowing absence. And she was relieved, vastly relieved, that what had been asked was in her power to give. This, after all, did not happen often.

2

Las Vegas, a city that veered so precipitously between the ridiculous and the hideous, how could it not feel like "home" to Virginia? All her homes had veered exactly that way, from the ridiculous to the hideous—first the home of her mother and father, then the home of her husband, and finally the home of that person who called himself, seemed to insist on calling himself, her "boyfriend," though he was neither a boy nor really a friend. But she was having trouble remembering any of those people. They faded in and out. She was having trouble remembering anyone—especially herself. She'd told someone, it might have been the psychiatrist, yes, it was, she'd said, "If you don't practice seeing yourself, you become invisible to yourself."

She defined her "illness," for that's what they insisted on calling it, as simply being out of practice. Out of practice at seeing herself. But now she thought that to *not* see herself had been a kind of practice for something else, something far more crucial. She was beginning to feel that it was good she couldn't see herself.

But she could see her feet. Which meant that once again she'd forgotten her shoes. Slipped them off her feet somewhere in that immense casino. In most places this wouldn't be a problem, or at least she wouldn't have considered it a problem, but in Las Vegas, in the summer, it *was* a problem because it was painful. That terrible sun made the pavement so hot. She'd tried to leave the casino, had gone not ten steps, and her feet really *hurt,* they were burning, and she'd run back in, run on the balls of her pretty feet, she thought her feet were pretty. They were quite dirty, but that was a nice touch, wasn't it? She thought of the word *gamin*. It was a word she'd always liked.

It would be all right if she didn't want to cry so much. She wanted to cry all the time now, wanted to, but couldn't quite remember how. It used to be easy, but not anymore. Which didn't seem like something she deserved. But she must deserve it, because it was so. That's how things worked, didn't they? Something final was needed, she remembered *that,* she couldn't get *that* out of her head.

There'd been a lot she hadn't wanted. She didn't want *this,* either, not really, but it was better than most other things she hadn't wanted. Freer. Nobody could say her name because nobody knew it anymore but her. If she had thought of doing *that* ten years ago, everything might have been all right.

"Are you *playing* that machine, lady?"

Virginia felt that questions shouldn't surprise her anymore, but she was almost always surprised, and she was annoyed at her surprise. She had been staring at her dirty feet, and this particular question made her aware, reluctantly, that she was sitting at a slot machine, the last of a long row of slot machines, among many many rows of many many slot machines, in a cacophonous place of bells and whistles and shouts and rattlings and sentence fragments overheard and colors that were far too bright and *lots* of people—not one of whom, to Virginia's eyes, seemed to belong there. This fact made her feel not so out of place, at last. And she liked the carpet. It had a swirly design and was colored a dull rouge mixed with blurry blues, and it felt good on the soles of her feet.

"*Are* you, lady?"

"I *am* a lady. What are you suggesting?"

He was a tall young man and he looked unhealthy. He wore cowboy boots and well-pressed jeans and an incongruous silk shirt of a color that Virginia decided was vermilion. It didn't go with the color of his skin, which was grayish. His eyes were uncertain, even a little afraid. Everybody's eyes seemed to be like that. It was a quality with which she was becoming impatient.

"I'm not . . . *suggesting* a thing, I don't think, I just want to play this machine if you're not going to, okay? It's the only free machine, I mean, on this row, I mean, if you're not using it. *Are* you?"

"It's not free. It costs a dollar. Have you got a dollar?"

"Lady . . . yes, I have a dollar."

"Well. Hand it over."

The tall young man suddenly smiled and his eyes stopped doing what they'd been doing. His eyes were interested in something else now, but Virginia couldn't tell what.

"That's pretty good," he said. "That's maybe the best panhandle line I've heard. Okay. *Okay.* Here."

He gave her a dollar token and she put it in the machine and pulled the lever. The machine started to make a lot of noise.

"Now *that's* luck," the young man said. "That's crazy luck."

A lot of dollar tokens were making a lot of noise, clanging and rattling out of the machine into the shiny trough that caught them.

"A hundred dollars ain't bad, lady."

Virginia got up. The noise was making her tired. The young man was making her tired. Whatever he was interested in seemed very far away. So did he. How could there be so many people who were so very far away? What were they far away *from?*

"Where's the church?" she said. "There's a church here, I saw it. I think I did. Where is it?"

"The wedding chapel?" He pointed vaguely in a direction that seemed impossibly distant to Virginia. "I think it's down that way."

Virginia got up and faced in the direction he'd pointed.

"Don't you want your money? I'll split it with you. It'd be bad luck *not* to. Fifty bucks ain't hay."

"It's not final enough. Neither are you."

3

There was very little left of her. That was both good and bad. Bad, because the feeling made her a little dizzy, and if she got dizzy enough she'd fall, and if she fell she knew what would happen and it wouldn't be final, it would just be more of the same. But good, too, because though by rights she should have been noticed and ejected, she somehow wasn't. She felt like a kind of wish, a walking wish, a thin flimsy sort of wish, and it wasn't a strong enough wish for anyone to notice, much less deny. In the ridiculous shop she'd seemed very important, but in this cacophonous maze of far-away people her own far-awayness seemed to fit in somehow, so she was smaller, unimportant. Finding a name had been important, and, it seemed to Virginia, the Gloria-person had responded to that importance. Going toward what was final *should* be important, but finality just seemed to go unnoticed around here, as though people didn't believe there could be such a thing. But there had to be.

The place was like a circus and a traffic jam and a jukebox and a high school dance and a labyrinth and a prison all in one, with lots of clangings and whistlings and talk, and half-naked women carrying trays. The itch in her crotch was almost not an itch anymore, it was almost a pain. Her scalp itched too, but that was different. As she walked in the direction of the church, trusting she would find it sooner or later, she would have liked just to look at her feet, but then she would have bumped into everything. She didn't like looking at what she had to look at.

The sign said WEDDING CHAPEL in pink neon. She'd been taught that every church was for the wedding of Heaven and Earth, so she thought the sign appropriate and honest. As for the pink neon, it was like that shop, which also was appropriate. But she should have burned that book. Then maybe there would have been no names. Then everybody could start over.

What was it about too-sweet pinks and powder blues? This place too. Not many pews. Not many people prayed anymore, must be the reason—prayer had become so difficult, after all. And there was no cross. No cross was bad and good. Bad, because a cross was a kind of street sign, it pointed up and down *and* right and left, from a cross you could go anywhere. But it was good, too, that there was no cross, because all those directions now confused Virginia. They made her feel like just standing still and never moving again. That was final, but not the kind of final she'd been searching for.

But at least there were no worshipers here. She'd wished for that and it had come true. It seemed the first place in a long time that she'd had all to herself. There was only the intrusion of that tinny, jingly music. Its source was unspecific, which, for such music, seemed more than appropriate. But she had learned to ignore almost everything, so she very soon ignored the music.

Perhaps she had sinned in not burning the book of names. Perhaps she'd had a chance to save the world, and had lost it. Perhaps the world had been depending on her for a chance to start clean. How could the life in her start cleanly with a name, any name, even Virginia? Nobody stays a Virginia for long. But not burning the book, that was a sin of omission, not a sin of commission. But perhaps those were the worst, the sins of omission. So much was omitted, everywhere, perhaps *that* was the sin of which, all her life, she'd been so afraid.

If she sat here long enough she'd be nameless. Yes, that was it. That would be final. And clean. And it *must* be possible. All that was required was a prayer that could not be remembered, not by her, not by anyone. Well. She would sit until she could remember it. Nobody would find her here, nobody cared about this place, that much was clear. She had forgotten so much already. It couldn't take much longer to forget everything. And once everything was forgotten, the baby could be born. There would be one clean unremembered place, unburdened by memory, for a new life to grow. Well, she'd found something then. And she felt the name Virginia leave her, it had been a mistake to look for a name, Gloria had tried to tell her that. Now the book of names burned inside her. And prayer was a burning, wasn't it? Soon she could cry again. In a while. A little while. But now she felt herself smiling again, golden again, shining again. All that was required was to be nameless and to shine.

Afterword

TODD SCOTT MOFFETT & TINA D. ELIOPULOS

Recently, my family visited Red Rock Canyon, a natural resource west of Las Vegas. As during my previous trips to the canyon, I was struck by the odd optical illusion presented by the flame-red cliff face visible at the first Calico overlook, a mile along the scenic driving loop. When we approached the overlook, the round, rocky hill that gave rise to the cliff did not appear to be very large—no more than the size, perhaps, of a sand dune, especially when viewed against the backdrop of Mount Charleston, a twelve-thousand-foot-tall mountain. Even when we arrived at the overlook and Mount Charleston retreated to our left, the cliff face did not seem big: I could span the wash separating the cliff from the overlook, I thought, by throwing a stone. My first clue to the true size of the cliff came when I saw the climbers clinging to the face. They looked no bigger than ants. The illusion of the cliff's smallness faded further when we hiked along the trails leading into the wash. It took awhile—longer than I'd thought it would—to descend to the dry riverbed. Then, when we reached the bottom, the cliff towered over us, a giant castle defending the foothills of the mountains.

The approach to Las Vegas presents me with a similar illusion, especially at night when the bright lights register the boundaries of the city. Descending into the valley from Apex or from Sloan, I see how small the city is, nestled below the mountains. It does not sprawl forever as does Seattle or Phoenix or Los Angeles but seems complete and contained within the valley walls. The casinos along the strip, too, seem colorful but distant, the size of the buildings I would set beside a model train set. The closer I come to the casinos, however, and the more I drive along the streets, the more I realize how large this city is. The facades of the casinos stretch longer than whole blocks would stretch in other cities, and the major intersections themselves are at least a mile apart. In my own neighborhood on the outskirts of Las Vegas, the illusion of size persists: when I make the short drive with my daughter to our local park, I realize again and again that the drive takes five minutes, that I've driven more than two miles—the distance between my house and my high school as I was growing up. A distance I used to think considerable.

The spatial illusions broadcast by Las Vegas and the surrounding landscape are at the same time an amusement that I would recommend and a warning that I would pass to newcomers. Enjoy them, but be wary of them. I have the same advice for those of you who read the stories that we have gathered for this collection. Many times, the stories will present you with images you think represent this city—gambling, bright lights, and the obsessive types who are addicted to both. But many times, too, the stories will present you with a view of Las Vegas that does not match up to your expectations.

Compiling these stories has helped me to view our city differently but has not solved the enigma I see at its heart. I don't expect these stories to solve any paradoxes for you, either, or make you appreciate our city any more than you do. I do hope, however, that they will make you realize that in some way you are part of the illusion, wherever you are. For what you think of the city wraps itself around each building, shadows each throw of the dice, and blows through the grass my daughter plays upon.

—T.S.M.

It was called "Mac's Manna," a short story set in the seventies about two twenty-something losers, Jebb, the redneck, and Mac, the hippie, from Kuna, Idaho, on spring vacation in Las Vegas. At his first try at gambling, Mac gets lucky playing keno and wins $3,500. Luck actually has nothing to do with it; Mac sits down next to the legendary comic Redd Foxx and picks the same numbers that Foxx is playing. Yes, as Mac giggles, high on weed, "I copied off of Mr. Sanford." Mac then decides that he and Jebb are destined for great fame, so they embark on a week of liquor, women, and more gambling. Their ultimate goal is to win enough cash so they can return home to Idaho and open a John Deere distribution center in Boise. Needless to say, they fall short of the happy ending: Mac is run over by an Elvis impersonator and Jebb falls in love with a hooker who breaks his heart.

There was nothing special about this short story; it was riddled with all those problems indicative of undergraduate creative writing: overwritten narrative, awkward pacing, stiff dialogue, and the melodramatic ending. However, when I submitted it to my creative writing instructor, Professor Robert Papinchak, who for nearly two semesters had told me that my writing was "dead, my god, is it dead," he actually smiled and said, "A Vegas story." Long pause. "What a great idea. There aren't too many of those." He was right. There weren't. There were the Vegas treatments, but there weren't the Las Vegas stories. Those few pieces written about the place were typically tossed off by those who had passed through the city or by those who had never even set foot here, but who had used the place's mystique to create their own world. When I'd tell my friends I'd be spending my summers in Las Vegas, each without fail would ask, "So, have you read *Fear and Loathing*?" Few knew this place.

Well, since that day, twenty years ago, things have changed. This city has doubled its population a few times over, built new parks, schools, and entire housing communities to accommodate all its new inhabitants, transformed the face of the Las Vegas Strip with one megaresort opening after another, sprouted its cultural wings, and become the refuge for Texans, New Yorkers, Californians, Floridians, and all those other former residents of states with winters too cold, housing prices too high, traffic too congested, taxes too consuming, earthquakes too devastating, and life mistakes too frequent. They've come here in equal numbers to start over, and to retire. And with these changes, this city has reinvented her national image. Las Vegas is no longer the town that Bugsy conquered, that Howard Hughes built, or that Elvis and Liberace loved. It now has the fingerprints of so many others on its grid. It purports to be the travel destination not just for high rollers and mobsters but for tourists from all over the globe. Bring your children, your golf clubs, your parents, your money, your suntan lotion, your in-laws, your neighbors, your dream. There is something here for everyone. Our tourist and redevelopment bureaus want those listening to hear this call. And many have. Those who have chosen to live here want this city to be safe, respectable, and respected; the people who live here—the number is approaching two million—want this city to be home.

At times, though, it can be an uncomfortable home. There's the gambling and its insidious stepchildren; there's the heat and its unrelenting presence; and there's the water and its eventual end. There are unhappy residents too, those same ones who came running to this city to save them. When they fail themselves, Las Vegas becomes their enemy. It's naturalism at its finest. No one ever thinks to blame a city like San Francisco—it's too lovely—or Denver—it's too rugged—or Boston—it's too old—or New York—it's too cultured—but folks will turn on Las Vegas in a heartbeat. Why? Well, Las Vegas, in spite of (or perhaps because of) her numerous reinventions, doesn't purport to be anything other than what she is. She cannot hide, and she cannot hide us, behind her geography, her weather, her history, her resources. Nor does she want to. For some of us, that's exactly why we stay; for others, it's why they flee. For the writers of the stories that appear in this anthology, it's this compelling paradox that in one way or another created their Las Vegas story. These aren't stories about losers from Idaho, these are stories about people who inhabit a very real place.

—T.D.E.

Contributors

H. LEE BARNES's short stories have appeared in numerous journals and magazines, including *Red Rock Review, Connecticut Review,* and *The MacGuffin.* He authored *Gunning for Ho: Vietnam Stories,* published by the University of Nevada Press, and has two books, *Dummy Up and Deal,* a nonfiction work released in 2002, and *Willy Bobbins,* a novel, due out in 2003. His work won the 1991 Arizona Authors Association and the 1997 *Clackamas Literary Review* (now the Willamette Award for Fiction) fiction awards. He teaches English at the Community College of Southern Nevada.

FELICIA CAMPBELL, Ph.D., is professor of English at UNLV, chair of the Asian Studies Program, executive director of the Far West Popular and American Culture Association, and book critic for KNPR public radio. She has published widely in areas from literature to popular culture to gambling behavior and is now working on final revisions of a short story collection.

ROBERT DODGE grew up in the small town of Cincinnatus, New York. He attended Rice University and the University of Texas, where he received a doctorate in English literature. Since 1970 he has taught at the University of Nevada, Las Vegas, where he is now a professor of English. His wife, Leslie, is also a writer of fiction. He has two children, Robert and Sarah.

DAYVID FIGLER is a municipal court judge in Clark County, Nevada. He has performed his off-kilter brand of humorous poetry/prose around the country since 1994. In 1998, he was awarded an artist fellowship from the Nevada State Arts Council and was named a Nevada Tumblewords Poet. His one-man show, *Dayvid Figler Is Jim Morrison in Hello, I Love You (Where You Folks From?),* sponsored by the City of Las Vegas, was selected as a feature on the literary stage at the 1999 Bumbershoot in Seattle, Washington. He is currently a featured commentator on KNPR (Nevada Public Radio).

ANDREW KIRALY is a native Las Vegan and associate editor of the alternative weekly the *Mercury.*"

DAVID KRANES is a writer of both dramatic and prose fiction. His stage plays have been performed in many major theaters in the United States and abroad. He is the author of five novels, including *The National Tree* (2001), and two books of stories. A novel, *Making the Ghost Dance*, is forthcoming, as is a new book of stories, *The Burning Lake*. His play *House, Bridge, Fountain, Gate* was presented at the Lark Theater in New York City in June 2001. He also consults with the casino industry in matters related to space and design. He retired early from teaching at the University of Utah in June 2001 to devote full time to his writing.

RICHARD LOGSDON, a college English professor living in Las Vegas, has taught at the Community College of Southern Nevada since 1975. He received his doctorate in English from the University of Oregon in 1976. He is the editor of three college textbooks, all published by Bellwether Press of Minnesota. Additionally, he has published short stories on and off the Web and enjoys writing dark fiction in his spare time. He is currently the editor of the small literary magazine *Red Rock Review.*

MATTHEW O'BRIEN is the managing editor for *CityLife,* a news and culture paper based in Las Vegas. He has published short stories, poems, and articles in various literary journals, magazines, and newspapers, including *Red Rock Review, SOMA,* and the *Las Vegas Review-Journal.* A native of Atlanta, Georgia, he has lived in Las Vegas since December 1997.

THOMAS A. PORTER is a writer living in Alaska.

GERMAN SANTANILLA was born in Colombia and moved to Las Vegas in 1964. He attended local schools and UNLV. He currently works as a Spanish interpreter/translator with the state and federal

district courts. His writing appeared in *Chance,* an Internet pub-
lication, and he is currently working on a novel, tentatively titled
The Motel.

DAVID SCOTT has played center field for the rookie league team
of the California/Anaheim Angels, surfed professionally in Hawaii
and Australia, and worked as an accountant for the Laguna Dam in
Yuma, Arizona. Currently, he is leading adventure tours in Nepal,
India, and Peru and is pursuing scholastic investigations into the
history of shamanism and its relation to the game of chess. His
greatest golfing moment came when he had to turn a golf club over
and swing left-handed to strike a ball lodged at the base of the tree;
the shot bounced twenty yards and landed in the cup.

JOSÉ SKINNER is the author of *Flight and Other Stories* published
by the University of Nevada Press. His short fiction has appeared in
*Red Rock Review, Quarterly West, Boulevard, Witness, Colorado Re-
view,* and other journals. For many years he worked as a Spanish-
English translator and interpreter. He is currently working on a
novel set in Central America.

JOHN L. SMITH is an award-winning columnist for the *Las Vegas
Review-Journal* and the author of *Running Scared: The Life and
Treacherous Times of Las Vegas Casino King Steve Wynn, On the
Boulevard,* and several other books. Born in Henderson, he traces
his family's roots in Nevada to 1881.

MICHAEL VENTURA's earliest essays on Las Vegas were included in
his first book, *Shadow Dancing in the USA,* in 1985. Since then his
observations on Las Vegas have appeared in *L.A. Weekly,* the *Los
Angeles Times, Las Vegas Life,* and *Psychology Today,* as well as in
other periodicals. One of his novels, *The Death of Frank Sinatra,* is,
in Michael's own words, "my psychological map of Vegas." He has
received many writing awards, but says, "The only one I've kept is
the one the Las Vegas City Council gave me [in December 1996] for
the *L.A. Times* piece."